MISTY WINTER

ALSO BY LINDA RAWLINS

Misty Point Mystery Series:

Misty Manor

Misty Point

Rocky Meadow Mystery Series:

The Bench

Fatal Breach

Sacred Gold

MISTY WINTER

A MISTY POINT MYSTERY

LINDA RAWLINS

Misty Winter

For Joseph B. Liotti

&

*All the animal lovers who work so hard
to rescue, care for, love and
prevent cruelty and suffering for animals everywhere.*

ACKNOWLEDGMENTS

Once again, I find myself grateful to so many people who have helped Misty Winter come to fruition. To my husband, Joseph B Liotti - Our many car rides, where characters and plots were discussed were not only productive but a lot of fun. Delivering my coffee while I fret about writing and editing at the computer is a gift beyond compare. Thanks for your support!

Many thanks to Noelle K Diana, DVM, MPH for help with all things veterinarian. All errors or misrepresentations are my own.

My first circle of readers – Joyce, Joe, Sandy, Anita, and Claire. You all do such a great job!

My hardest editor – Krista O'Neill who does an excellent job with my manuscript and blurbs.

My producer – Matthew J. Liotti who does a great job with my covers, website, and promotion as well as Ashley who helps support all!!

My many readers, librarians and friends - your enthusiasm and encouragement inspire me on a daily basis. Thank you for reading and sharing my stories.

CHAPTER 1

"Don't be afraid. I promise this won't hurt a bit," Dr. Arnie Stokes said as he held the animal against the cold metal table and swept the nearby syringe into his hand. He spent a few minutes trying to calm the puppy as he gently stroked his fur but the chilly air wafting through the clinic didn't help. When the trembling stopped, the veterinarian placed the plastic cap of the hypodermic between his teeth, pulled the syringe free and slid the tip of the sharp, sterile needle under the puppy's skin. Pressing the plunger, he then removed the needle and rubbed the injection site for a second before he let the creature go.

With a small shake, the animal stood and looked at the veterinarian with big brown eyes.

"See, that wasn't so bad." Dr. Stokes smiled at the puppy and grabbed the small leash attached to a metal ring on the edge of the table. He gingerly lifted the dog and placed him on the floor. "I know, it's been a long day. Time to get some rest." Wobbling, the dog walked down the aisle, past numerous cages which held kittens, puppies, and rabbits. The next room hosted larger animals in the infirmary or those being watched in the kennel while their owners were away.

Near the back, several older dogs waited patiently for adoption and their forever homes.

"You'll feel much better soon," Dr. Stokes said as he led the dog to his assigned cage. "Everyone hates immunizations, but they protect you against certain diseases." As they paraded through the clinic, other animals reacted by jumping or scratching at their cage. Some of the dogs barked and cats cried out. A few remained curled up on towels.

Dr. Stokes opened the cage door, unclipped the leash and ushered the dog inside. He placed a small bowl of dry food near the back and closed the door, twisting the lock so the puppy couldn't escape.

"There you go, that should hold you for the night." As he walked back to the exam table, the animals continued to yelp, bark and cry out for attention so he turned off the overhead lights hoping it would help them quiet down and rest.

Intent on cleaning the exam room, Dr. Stokes picked up the empty vial and used syringe. He placed them in the medical waste container and proceeded to wipe the table with a scented antiseptic. In preparation for an operation in the morning, he located a surgical instrument pack and placed it on a sterile tray with a cover to maintain its cleanliness.

As he continued to prepare, he got lost in his thoughts about the clinic. He had to finish the budget and reapply for the Stanford Grant to keep the Hand in Paws Animal Clinic open. He was worried about the funding. Rose Stanford had always been generous in the past, but since she passed away, he would have to present to new members of the board of directors and Dr. Stokes knew they would ask questions. Accountability for money, supplies, and adoptions was complicated enough, but what if someone started asking questions about the break-ins and thefts over the last six months?

Dr. Stokes wanted to handle the problem quietly by identifying the culprit and calling the police. He hadn't realized the cameras weren't working. After the second robbery, the veterinarian pulled the security footage to see who had been in the clinic and was dismayed to find the video was blank. He checked the cameras and found each one had a broken lens and was not capable of recording events. Instead of going to the board members, Dr. Stokes kept quiet in hopes of a miracle. He didn't want to explain why the cameras weren't working and more importantly admit his role in not reporting various crimes surrounding the Stanford Grant.

Lost in his thoughts, Dr. Stokes jumped when he heard a loud sneeze as he entered the supply room. Startled, he turned toward the intruder. After a small pause, he gathered himself and said, "You scared me. I didn't hear you come in."

"Sorry about that. I came to check on some of the animals."

"That's very kind, but certainly not necessary. I've been with them most of the day. They've been fed and accounted for. We certainly appreciate our volunteers, but we don't expect you to work extra-long hours."

"It's no problem, doctor. I didn't realize you were working this late or I wouldn't have disturbed you."

"No harm done," Dr. Stokes said as he glanced around the room. He looked back at the volunteer, his suspicions beginning to rise. "Is there anything I can help you with?"

"No, not at all." The volunteer shifted his weight as well as the many supplies he was holding.

"You look like you have your hands full. What have you got there?"

The volunteer said nothing and stood still. He didn't smile or explain why he was standing in the supply room after hours.

Dr. Stokes clenched his jaw. "You're the one who's been stealing all the supplies and expensive meds. Why? What are you doing with all this stuff?"

The volunteer slowly put everything down on a nearby shelf.

Dr. Stokes tried again. "Are you selling it? I'll give you five minutes to explain but then I'm calling the police. You can tell them."

Grabbing the doctor's arm, the volunteer said, "You're going nowhere, and you'll keep your mouth shut." He reached inside his jacket, pulled out a 9mm Glock and brandished it in front of the doctor's face.

Pulling his arm free, Dr. Stokes took a step backward. "What do you want?" His eyes darted around the room looking for a means of escape.

"A lot of things. I think you have an idea what's going on here and now I think you're in the wrong place at the wrong time, which is a big problem."

Dr. Stokes blanched as he watched his intruder. He backed up another step and said, "It doesn't have to be a problem. Just go, take whatever you want and leave. I won't say anything, I promise."

"Thank you, but I'm afraid that arrangement won't work out. I'm not the only one involved in this operation."

Dr. Stokes laughed nervously as he reached behind his back to grab one of the disposable scalpels from the shelf. "What operation? As far as I'm concerned, it's just some stolen supplies. It happens all the time."

The volunteer remained quiet while Dr. Stokes swallowed hard. "What good would it do to kill me? Who'll take care of the animals and the clinic?"

"I'm sure someone will replace you. I wouldn't waste time worrying about it."

As the intruder raised the gun, Dr. Stokes jumped forward and shoved the blade of the scalpel into the side of the intruder's neck. He quickly turned, ran out of the supply room and into the main clinic. Behind him, a scream reached his ears, as well as noise from frenzied animals as something crashed to the floor. Running down an aisle, he hit a display with his hip as he looked backwards for his assailant. Staggering behind him was the volunteer, shirt starting to pool with blood. Several bullets whipped by Dr. Stokes's head as samples of heart worm pills flew about the room. Leaning forward, he ran toward the back door but stopped short when the tip of a 9mm bullet hit his back, shattering his spine. Sliding toward the floor, his last vision, before he lost consciousness, was a pair of large, brown, puppy eyes staring at him through a cage door.

CHAPTER 2

*M*egan Stanford stood, hands on hips, and surveyed the pile before her. She leaned down, retrieved an item and held it in the air. "Georgie, what do you think of this lamp?"

"I wouldn't want it, but other than that, I have no idea."

"I'll put it in the appraiser pile. Let's see what he has to say."

"Any word from the architect?" Georgie asked.

Megan placed the lamp on the other side of the room, turned and looked at her friend from high school. "He made an appointment to come tomorrow. I'm a little nervous about what he'll find, and the price tag attached, but I promised to listen."

"He's a specialist in historic renovation and restoration, with a focus on Grand Victorian homes, so he's bound to be expensive."

"We'll see," Megan said with a frown as she went back to sorting a pile of furnishings the two women had pulled from the third floor earlier in the day.

"I want to refurbish Misty Manor, but I don't know about historic renovation," Megan said as she shook her head. "That sounds like a big, expensive project."

Georgie laughed. "The bigger the words, the more expensive the bill."

"So very true."

"What are your plans after you talk to the appraiser?"

Megan paused for a moment. "I'm not sure. I guess it depends on the value he places on the things we show him. Maybe he can sell some items on consignment." Megan continued to sort through the pile before her.

"What about an estate sale?" Georgie asked.

Megan turned and shook her head. "Definitely not. I don't want any curiosity seekers in Misty Manor. I had enough grief with Abigail and her sticky fingers."

"Yes, but she didn't get anything as far as we know."

"I'm not sure about that. I never got the chance to search her suitcase," Megan said as she shrugged her shoulders.

Georgie smiled at her friend. "Have you heard anything about your unwanted visitors since they went back to Texas?"

"Not a word and I like it that way," Megan said as she went back to her pile and continued to sort. "I can't believe my father invited them to Misty Manor. Thankfully, they weren't successful when they tried to change Grandma Rose's will."

As they worked in silence, Megan thought of the special memories she held from growing up in Misty Manor. Her grandmother, Rose, had practically raised Megan from a child, while her parents played out a dysfunctional relationship which finally culminated in a separation that sent her mother fleeing. Once Megan was done with high school, she left home to go to college and never returned. She had been gone quite a few years.

Six months prior, Megan lost her job as a journalist for the Detroit Virtual News. The same day, she received a call from her father, Dean, asking her to return to New Jersey to take care of her dying grandmother. He was unaware of her job loss, but simply called because Rose had continued to decline, and he was too busy in Europe with his paramour, Gigi, to come back and take care of her. Dean was an angry, narcissistic, resentful man who wanted nothing except adoration and monetary gain.

Having nowhere else to go, Megan returned to New Jersey and

took on the responsibility of caring for Rose during the last few months of her life. Megan now realized how much she had missed her grandmother and Misty Manor, the Grand Victorian in which she grew up. Staying away from home had been Megan's way of avoiding the ugly realities of her childhood. She was sorry she hadn't spent more time with her grandmother after college and felt guilty about not returning to thank her for raising and loving her.

A strong woman, Rose Stanford was wealthy and owned over half of the town of Misty Point but instead of flaunting her power and influence, she focused on helping others.

Rose had passed several months ago. As a result, Megan had inherited the means and passion to bring the Grand Victorian back to its former glory. In addition to her inheritance, Megan had committed to continue her grandmother's philanthropy and support the many Stanford Grants and charities throughout the area.

"Penny for your thoughts?" Georgie asked, as she threw a pillow over to Megan.

Megan shrugged. "Nothing specific, just reliving some of the memories I've had in Misty Manor."

"That's fine, but don't dwell on it," Georgie said with a smile. "It's time to make new memories. We'll help you bring the house back to life."

Megan laughed as she looked at her friend. "That's what I'm worried about."

Georgie threw a towel at her and turned back to her pile. "Are you sure you don't want to have an estate sale?"

"Yes, I'm sure," Megan admitted. "I don't need to raise money and I want to keep anything that was valuable to Rose. I'm only getting rid of worthless old items right now."

"Speaking of things valuable to Rose, when are we going to peek in that attic?" Georgie asked as she dusted off her hands by wiping them on her pants.

"Soon," Megan said, "Christmas is almost here, and I was thinking of putting up some of the vintage decorations before the holiday."

"Finally," Georgie said with a huge smile. "Thanksgiving was a bust this year. You now own a gorgeous four story Grand Victorian on the point of this glorious town. Misty Manor hasn't seen decorations for years, but it used to be a tradition when we grew up. Everyone walked down the boardwalk to see the special Christmas decorations at Misty Manor." Georgie laughed at the memory. "I think we were the only town who had an organized Ocean Holiday Walk just to see the lights and decorations reflecting off the water. I loved that walk. It always ended in the town square with the annual tree lighting."

"And lots of Christmas cookies and hot chocolate," Megan said with a laugh. "Some years were warm enough that we'd walk in the water instead of on the boardwalk."

"Yea, and some years, we'd freeze our butts off in that ocean wind. The Atlantic off the Jersey Coast can be fickle in the winter time."

Megan smiled at the memory. "Wow, that was a long time ago. I remember my grandmother started that tradition when we were in grade school."

"And it continued straight through high school," Georgie said picking up another pillow.

Megan looked at her friend. "Did that stop because of Hurricane Sandy?"

Georgie paused. "No," she said as she shook her head slowly. "The walk continued for a few years after you left for college, but really fizzled out when you didn't come home. I don't want to make you feel bad, but I think Rose was getting older and without family around, she just lost heart. We stopped having the walk a few years before Sandy hit the area but that was a particularly bad winter at the beach."

"What was it like?"

Georgie sat on the end of the couch and shook her head. "Bad, it was really bad. The storm hit at the end of October 2012. I can't believe it's been five years now. The governor had ordered a manda-tory evacuation, and for good reason. Hurricane Sandy caused massive destruction everywhere from the Caribbean straight up to Canada. I think about 150 people died, but the thing I remember most of all was that it was dark, very dark until we were able to get power restored to the area." Georgie looked up at her friend. "It was scary for a while. Roads were blocked, no electricity, no food or gas coming in. A lot of homes were destroyed. Most of us lived somewhere else for months before we could return. Hell, some people still haven't returned. Anyway, there were very few lights on that year, at all."

When Georgie looked up, the sadness in Megan's eyes broke her heart.

Georgie hugged her friend. "I'm sorry, we shouldn't be talking about that."

"No, it's alright. I was thinking about Rose and how she must have felt during the disaster. I'm sure it was frightening, especially at her age," Megan said. "I didn't come back to New Jersey, but I know Rose evacuated for a brief time. Of course, Virtual News covered the storm and destruction. We worked day and night to keep up with the devastation, despite the fact we were in Detroit. That was the excuse I used for not coming home." Megan swallowed as she continued. "I kept calling to find her and finally got a message through a social worker she was okay. She'd moved into an assisted living facility for a short time, but returned to Misty Manor as soon as she was physically able. The house was in disrepair, but she survived." A tear trickled down Megan's cheek. "She was an amazingly strong woman. I miss her so much."

Georgie dropped everything she was holding, walked over and hugged her friend. "The best thing you can do is honor her memory by bringing Misty Manor back to life."

Megan nodded as she wiped her cheek. "Hey, maybe we could restart some of the traditions around here. What do you think?"

"That would be great," Georgie said. "Let's get everyone on board, especially Amber. She could get all sorts of corporate sponsors."

"We could try to decorate Misty Manor and if it looks good, we could restart the Ocean Holiday Walk, and some of the activities in the town square," Megan said, hope rising in her heart.

"Better watch out," Georgie warned. "You're actually looking excited about this idea."

"I think it's a great idea. Misty Point needs some rejuvenation. We have to form a committee."

"Like grandmother, like granddaughter," Georgie said as she shook her head and rolled her eyes.

"Oh, shut up. We'll get a lot more accomplished if we get other people from the town involved."

Laughing, Georgie said, "I agree but we have a problem."

"And that is?"

"Your buddy, our esteemed mayor, Andrew Davenport."

Megan frowned. "Oh, that jerk. He doesn't make all the decisions around town. We can go through the town council or the recreation committee. I'm sure they would love to restore some wonderful traditions to this town."

"As long as they have the money. There may not be enough in the budget."

"I can talk to Teddy about the Stanford Grants," Megan said. "After all, as Rose's lawyer, he's been involved in these grants and committees for years. I'm sure they can come up with a few bucks for a special project like this."

Georgie smiled and went back to her work. "C'mon, we've got to get through this pile if we want to be able to spend time making plans."

Megan laughed. "With pleasure."

CHAPTER 3

"*There's* a lot of blood on this wall," Nick Taylor said as he looked around the small room at the back of the Hand in Paws clinic.

"The CSI techs will take samples and see who it belongs to," Chief Davis said as he scribbled findings on a pad. He turned toward Nick. "Tell me again how this call came in."

Nick straightened up and looked at his Chief. "There was a couple walking by the clinic. All the lights were on and the animals were barking and crying out. The couple have lived in this neighborhood for a long time and felt it was unusual activity for the time of night. The guy walked around back, saw the door was open and the good doctor on the ground. He called 911 and here we are."

Davis nodded as he listened. "How is the vic?"

"He's in surgery at Coastal Community. I haven't heard anything yet."

"Not to be sarcastic but does your girlfriend have anything to do with this clinic?" Davis asked.

"Are we going to start picking on Megan again?" Nick said defensively.

"Hey, I don't want to pick on anyone's love life. It's just interesting we've had two dead bodies and now a shooting since Megan Stanford came back to town and she's been connected to every case."

Nick crossed his muscular arms in front of him. "Since Megan has inherited Misty Manor and the board chair to all her grandmother's grants and charities, I imagine she'll be connected to most everything. Hell, Rose Stanford owned more than half the town and donated a boatload of money to many charities and left most of it to Megan, as far as I know."

"Interesting," Davis said. "And you're conveniently there to pronounce your love."

"You're an ass," Nick said as he frowned and turned back to the crime scene. He had been in love with Megan in high school, asked her to the prom and was crushed when she turned him down to go with the mayor's son. His "so-called" friends assured him that was normal when you lived on the wrong side of the tracks, but the pair had reconnected when Megan moved back to the Jersey Shore six months ago. Nick was still crazy about Megan, but wanted to take it slow and make sure she was happy. Since Megan inherited her grandmother's estate, people assumed he was chasing her for her money, which totally pissed him off.

"You run this guy's license yet?" Davis asked Nick. "Any criminal background or reason someone would be out for his head?"

"None that I could find," Nick shouted above the noise in the room. The animals in the clinic were spooked by the police activity. Officers were roaming through the place, looking for clues. EMS had been there earlier to collect Dr. Arnie Stokes and transport him to the emergency room. Outside, on the lawn, curiosity seekers had gathered to gawk at the scene. Officer Peters was taking a statement from the couple who had called 911. The animals were becoming more agitated as each hour of the investigation went by.

"Hello? What's going on?" Officer Nick Taylor and Chief Davis turned simultaneously to see a plump woman come through the back door of the clinic. Dressed in a green smock embroidered with a set of paws, she had light brown hair and dimples in each check.

Nick stepped forward. "Sorry ma'am, you can't be in here, this is a crime scene."

"A what?" The woman blanched at his words.

"Please, ma'am, you need to step outside," Nick said as he began to guide her to the door.

"They called me down here," the woman said as Davis watched from across the room. She appeared nervous. Eyes wide she tried to look around Nick.

Nick stepped to the side to block her view. "What's your name?"

The woman shook her head as if she couldn't hear above the ruckus from the animals. Nick took his pad out of his pocket and asked in a louder voice. "Can I have your name?"

"Judy Bowan," she said as she watched Nick write it down. "There's an a after the w. You put an e." She beamed a proud smile at him.

Nick stopped and looked up at her without expression. "Thank you, ma'am. Who called you down here?"

"I'm not sure," Judy said. "But they wanted me to come help with the animals."

"Do you normally work here?" Nick asked.

"I'm one of the volunteers," Judy said in a sweet voice. "We have many animal lovers who come help us, but several months ago, they put me in charge of all the volunteers, so I guess that's why they called me."

"I see," Nick said as he turned and looked at Davis.

"Can you calm these animals down?" Davis asked.

"Well, eventually I suppose," Judy said as she shrugged. "There's a lot of activity in here. Are you almost done?"

Davis squinted at the feisty volunteer. "Not for a while, ma'am. Our investigators have more work to do."

Judy frowned as she surveyed the room. "It's late, so they should be settling down, but they won't do that until the lights go off and the sound quiets down. Have they been fed? The poor animals are scared," Judy said as she leaned forward to check the officer's badge, "Chief Davis."

Nick chuckled and turned his face as Davis reddened. "I appreciate that, ma'am."

"Oh please, call me Judy," she said with a big smile.

Davis continued to shuffle. He cleared his throat. "Yes, ah... Judy."

"Will you be done with the front room soon? Then we could close the door and turn the lights out in the one room. But we can't fit all the animals in there."

"Well, ma'am, I mean, Judy," Davis said. "Who's your boss?"

Judy looked at the Chief and tilted her head. "My boss?"

"Yes, who gives you direction? Who oversees the clinic?"

"Well, Dr. Arnie Stokes, of course."

"And when Dr. Stokes goes on vacation? Who covers then?"

Judy paused for a moment. "I don't quite know, because he never seems to go away. Is he alright?"

"Someone must be listed in case of emergency," Davis tried again.

Judy shrugged and shook her head. "The only thing I know is the clinic runs on a Stanford Grant. Beyond that, I have no idea who's in charge other than Dr. Stokes."

Davis nodded. "Okay, stay right here and don't touch anything. I'll see if the crew is done in the front room. If they are, you'll be able to start calming the animals in there."

"What about the ones back here?" Judy asked.

"I'm going to get someone to help you," Davis said as he shifted his weight.

Judy's eyes opened wide. "You're not sending them to animal control or the pound, are you? That would be very upsetting. I can call more of the volunteers to help."

"Absolutely not," Davis shook his head. "This is a crime scene. I'm not letting anyone else enter this building. I'm not even sure how you got in here."

"A crime scene?" Judy asked, her voice rising again. "You keep saying that. Where is Dr. Stokes? Is it safe?"

"Yes, it's secure now." He looked directly at Judy. "Stay right here. Don't move or touch anything."

When she nodded her head, he pulled Nick to the side. "Go up front and see if they've cleared that room. If so, our friendly volunteer, Judy, can check the place and see if anything else looks amiss."

Nick nodded. "Got it."

"Then I want you to call your girlfriend and get her down here."

"Why?" Nick asked, tilting his chin.

"If she's in charge of the grant that runs this place, we need to talk to her. She can also find a way to get the animals out of this room. It's a crime scene. I can't let a bunch of volunteers trample the place, so get her down here."

Nick bristled at his Chief's derisive words, but realized it was the proper thing to do. He scowled, nodded his head and went to talk to the CSI's in the front of the clinic.

CHAPTER 4

*M*egan stood up straight and dusted her hands off as she turned to her friend. "Georgie, I can't thank you enough for coming today. You've been an immense help."

Georgie placed the last piece of bric-a-brac in the living room and nodded. "Honestly, I only agreed for the pizza and beer. The rest of this annoys me."

Megan burst out laughing. "You did not." She would have said more but turned when she heard the phone ring. "Who the heck would be calling me at this time of night?"

"I'm sure it's one of the many telemarketers who frequent our phones." Georgie raised her hands over her head and stretched. "All this bending is making me stiff."

Megan looked at her friend and laughed. "Yeah, right. You're in better shape than all of us. You work out every day."

"I've got to. We've got lifeguard tournaments coming up in the Spring. You can't stop training during the winter. Some of these kids are really good and I'm proud to be their Chief."

"Kids?"

"I call them kids. They're all in college. Let's face it, you, me and all our friends are pushing thirty, so they seem young to me."

"Which is why it's important they have a good mentor like you. They have youth and maybe they have brains, but there's a lot to be said for experience in this world."

"True, I can coach them but it's getting harder to keep up with them. I have one guard who is fantastic at Beach Flags."

"I don't remember all the rules for that," Megan said as she frowned. "I guess I've been away from the shore too long."

Georgie smiled. "See, your memory is going already. It's what we do to practice sprinting and reflexes on the sand. Sort of like musical chairs at the beach. We plant less flags than competitors. There's a complete set of rules, but basically, if you don't capture a flag you get eliminated."

"Now, I remember. You were pretty good at that, but your strength was always the surfboat."

"I love the surfboat challenge," Georgie said but before she could comment further, Megan's cell phone began to chime again.

"Again? Where did I put my phone?" Megan looked around the clutter as she followed the chime. "Found it." She picked up the cell and checked the screen. "It's Nick. I hope everything's alright." Hitting the green button, she answered his call. "Hi, Nick."

"Megan, I'm glad I got you," Nick said in a rush. "I tried calling earlier, but you didn't pick up."

"Oh, sorry about that. Georgie and I were going through some things at Misty Manor. Is everything ok?"

"No, not exactly. We've got a problem. Are you familiar with the Hand in Paws Animal Clinic?"

Megan paused for a second. "I think I've passed it, but I've never been in there."

"There was a shooting there, tonight. The veterinarian who worked there is in surgery at Coastal Community and his condition is critical. We're at the clinic to process the crime scene."

"Oh, no. Do you know who did it?"

"No, not yet. Megan, I need you to come down here."

"Me? Why?"

"The animals are very unsettled, and we still have a lot of work to do. The volunteer manager is here but we need to talk to someone in authority."

"Do you need me to come down and help with the pets?" Megan asked.

"No, I need you to come here as the authority."

Megan was silent for a moment. "What are you saying, Nick? I'm confused."

"From what we can tell, the clinic is run by a Stanford Grant. The only authority above the veterinarian here is the board of directors who oversee the place and since you inherited your grandmother's role, as board chair, that means you."

"Me? I don't know anything about it. I haven't sat down with Teddy to go over the various committees and grants yet."

"Well, then I suggest you call him, because we need to get some information about the Hand in Paws clinic and we need it soon."

"Okay," Megan paused to think for a moment. "Nick, give me a minute to call him and then I'll come down."

"Excellent, see you soon," Nick said. His voice then softened, and he added, "Love you."

Megan felt her face blush as she smiled. "Love you, too."

Georgie stood near her friend, arms folded in front of her waiting to hear the news. "What was that all about?"

Megan searched through her contacts list as she answered, "Apparently, the vet who runs the Hand in Paws clinic was shot tonight and they want to speak to me as a representative of the board."

"A shooting in Misty Point? That's kind of scary."

"I know," Megan agreed as she looked up. "We never had violence like that in town when we were younger. I don't know if it was targeted or not, but I have to go down there."

"Do you want me to come with you?"

"Sure, if you don't mind," Megan said. "They may not let you in, but they may need help with the animals."

"Then, let's go," Georgie said as she turned to grab her bag.

"Okay, but first I need to call Teddy."

"Well, get to it, so we can get down there and help."

"Already started," Megan said as she found his contact information and dialed.

CHAPTER 5

Theodore Harrison Carter, known to the family as Teddy, was the estate attorney, having served as Rose Stanford's legal counsel for years. He was the most familiar with her assets, charities and accounts, all of which were inherited by Megan upon Rose's death. The estate was worth over two hundred million dollars which caused Megan to pass out when she was told. Her friends were aware she inherited Misty Manor, but were not made aware of it's worth. Inherited along with the estate were the various responsibilities overseen by Rose. She had wanted to keep her philanthropic legacy alive as it served so many needs and would be thrilled beyond the grave to know that Megan had agreed.

Driving toward the clinic with Georgie in the passenger seat, Megan was surprised when she turned the corner and saw all the activity on the street. Multiple police cars with flashing lights, people standing on the lawn and an investigator van were all haphazardly arranged on the block before her.

"Wow, they're not fooling around with this, are they?" Georgie asked as she let out a low whistle.

"Apparently not," Megan said as she pulled her car to the side of the road. The pair got out of the car and walked toward the clinic.

They walked up to the officers near the back door but were told to stop before they got there.

"Excuse me, but I was called down here," Megan said to one of the officers. "I need to talk to Officer Nick Taylor of the Misty Point Police Department."

"And your names are?" The officer asked as he sized the pair up.

"I'm Georgie," she said awkwardly as she pointed at Megan. "I'm a friend of hers."

"I'm Megan Stanford and I really need to talk to Nick."

"Megan? As in Nick's girlfriend?" The officer asked, a smile now crossing his face.

Megan blushed, but nodded. "I guess so."

"Nick talks about you all the time."

"Oh, really?" Georgie asked. "That's interesting."

"Wait right here. I'll go find Nick."

"Thank you," Megan said as she elbowed Georgie who was about to say something else.

"What?" Georgie asked with an expression of pure innocence. "I'm trying to help here."

Megan didn't answer but turned when she heard her name. Nick was near the door of the clinic waving them over. Once they reached the door, Nick stepped outside for a second and gave Megan a quick kiss on the cheek. "Thanks for getting here so quickly. Chief Davis is ranting inside. He wants info and he wants it quick."

"Nick, I'll do the best I can, but I don't know very much about the clinic."

"Did you call Teddy?" Nick whispered as he grabbed her hand.

"Yes. He told me to call him when I see Davis for any general questions, but Teddy will have to go to his office tomorrow for any detailed information."

"That's good enough to start," Nick said. "Okay, let's go in." He turned to Georgie. "I'm going to have to ask you to stay out here. It's a crime scene inside and we must limit traffic to essential people only. But stay around because we need your help with these animals."

"They sound awfully upset," Megan said as she listened to the barking inside.

Georgie nodded as she looked at Nick. "Sure, I came with Megan, so I have to stay as long as she does."

"Thanks, I appreciate it." Nick turned back toward Megan and guided her through the door. They stepped to the side and waited until Chief Davis acknowledged them. After shouting orders, he finally walked toward them, his face dark with anger.

"Miss Stanford, thank you for coming." He gestured to the room behind him. "As you can see, we've had a shooting and we're getting nowhere fast with this investigation. I need some information about the Hand in Paws clinic and the only person who can help me right now is you."

"I'd be happy to help, Chief, but I don't have much information either. I did call Teddy and he told me to dial him when I got here. He has some history of the clinic and can get you started in the right direction."

Davis nodded toward her cell phone. "Then dial and let's get moving on this."

Megan punched in the numbers and listened to the ring while she waited for Teddy to pick up.

Teddy finally answered. "You've reached Theodore Harrison Carter. How may I be of assistance?"

"Teddy, it's me. I'm with Chief Davis and he'd like to speak with you."

"But, of course. Please put him on."

Megan handed her cell phone to Davis who walked away from the animals, so he could hear better.

When he was far enough away, Megan turned to Nick and whispered, "What the heck happened here? The place is wild."

"We're still not sure. We got a call and when the officers responded, they found Dr. Stokes face down. He'd been shot in the back. It looks like there was a struggle. Unfortunately, none of the animals are talking," Nick said as he smiled at Megan.

"In a way, they are," Megan laughed as she looked around. "Just not in your language."

"We have a volunteer up front, trying to soothe some of them, but they're still agitated. In the meantime, we've got to figure out what happened, before we can understand why."

Nick and Megan jumped when they heard a loud voice at their side. "What in the hell is going on here? Where's Davis?"

Nick glanced over to see Mayor Andrew Davenport at the doorway. Nick moved to intercept him before he entered the building and trampled over potential evidence. "Chief Davis is taking a report, sir, he'll be back in a second. I need to ask you to wait here."

Davenport glared at the officer's badge. "Taylor? I should have known." He then turned around and saw Megan standing on the side. "What's she doing in here?"

"Chief Davis asked her to come down for informational purposes." As he explained, the Chief walked over to the small group of people. Before Davenport opened his mouth, Davis cut him off and Megan sidled closer, so she could listen in.

"I just got off the phone with the Stanford attorney," Chief Davis said as he acknowledged Davenport, looking him up and down.

"It figures she's involved with this circus," Davenport said in a huff.

"She's not personally involved as far as I know," Davis shot back. "The clinic is run by a Stanford Grant, which helps the town with animal control immensely. The veterinarian is employed through the grant. Apparently, there's not an executive director between the doctor and the grant so we called Ms. Stanford down here to help us out."

"What kind of help?" Davenport asked. "What's going on?"

"Dr. Stokes was shot in the back, but not before there was a scuffle. We're trying to piece together what happened here tonight."

"Is this something the whole town needs to worry about?"

"Don't know if it was random or not," Davis said. "We had the volunteer supervisor look around, but it doesn't appear anything is missing."

Davenport frowned. "Well, figure it out before we have the media involved. I don't want a repeat of what happened this summer. That was all your fault, too," he said as he pointed at Megan. He looked back toward Davis. "You know where to find me." Davenport turned and walked out the back door. He crossed the property and scurried to his car before anyone could stop him and ask questions.

"He's just a ray of sunshine, isn't he?" Megan asked as they watched him go. Turning back toward Davis she said, "Was Teddy able to help you with the information you needed?"

"He had a few answers, but he'll have to call me tomorrow after he's had a chance to pull the grant information."

Realizing she knew nothing about the clinic, Megan made a mental note to arrange a meeting to learn more about the causes she was responsible for.

"Excuse me, please." The group turned around to see Judy smiling at Davis.

"Can I help you?" The Chief asked.

"Yes, I was just wondering if you had any more information as to what's happening tonight. Being December and all, it's starting to get cold in here. Can we close the door, so the animals don't start to shiver?"

Davis looked around as if realizing for the first time it was a chilly, dark, December night.

Judy continued. "Perhaps we can close the front door of the clinic, so we can keep that room warm and quiet."

Davis studied Judy for a moment before answering. "I'll check with my team to see if they're done in there."

Megan couldn't help but smile as she watched Davis speak with Judy. She elbowed Nick in the side and nodded when he turned toward her. It was the first time Davis didn't reduce someone to tears.

"Thank you, kind sir," Judy said as she smiled at him. Nick had to stifle a laugh when he noticed his chief suck his gut in a bit. She continued, "Hopefully, that will work out, but even so, we have a few animals in the back and we won't be able to fit the cages in the other room." Judy turned to Megan. "Perhaps you can help, Dearie. Do you know anyone who can adopt a pet for a night or two until these fine gentlemen finish their investigation? I can send a few of them home with our volunteers, but they won't be able to take them all."

Megan smiled at Judy's rosy face. Her wide grin was infectious. "I don't know too many people, but my friend is right outside. She probably knows quite a few people." Megan turned to Nick. "Can I call her to the door and ask?"

"Sure, as long as she doesn't come inside. She'd have to sign in."

Megan went to the door and signaled for Georgie to come near. When she was close, she brought Judy over and introduced her. Looking at Judy she said, "Go ahead, ask her. I'll bet she can help us."

"Oh, hello Miss. My name is Judy Bowan and I'm the manager for the volunteers here at the Hand in Paws Animal Clinic."

"Ah, hello?" Georgie said, confusion lining her face.

Pointing behind her, Judy said, "We have a little situation inside and the nice policemen have to do some official things in there." Georgie nodded politely as she listened. "The problem is we have to remove some of the animals from the room they're working in and we don't have any other room, so I was wondering if you knew anyone who would be willing to foster a pet for a brief time? All we need is a warm, caring place. Maybe for a week at most. What do you say?"

Georgie stammered for a few minutes. "I'm sorry, but I can't take any."

"I understand that, but do you happen to know anyone else who can? Take a moment and think about it." Judy's smile allowed the dimples pop out on her rosy cheeks. Behind her, Megan shrugged and raised her eyebrows in question.

"You know, I'll make a call to my mom," Georgie said. "She'd probably want to foster a pet and she'll know others who would foster as well."

"See, I knew Georgie would help us," Megan said triumphantly. When Judy turned to look at her, Georgie shot Megan a dirty look behind her back.

After fifteen minutes of phone calls, they were able to find temporary homes for all the animals in the back room. Georgie's mom and her friends each took a foster pet. The local assisted living facility asked if they could have a rabbit. They'd been looking for one to wheel around the facility to help with their pet therapy program and if all worked well, they planned on making it a forever home. The rest were taken home by the volunteers who were able to foster a dog. Within an hour, all the animals in the back room were claimed. The three women stayed at the clinic until each pet had been fed and had their blankets, beds, bowls, food, leashes or carriers properly loaded and strapped into the cars that would bring them to their new homes.

"Well, that went exceedingly well," Judy chirped excitedly. "I'm going to bet some of these foster adoptions will turn into permanent homes."

"I'm sure my mother will keep her dog," Georgie said as she turned to the group. "She loves dogs."

"Now, we only have one more teeny-weeny problem," Judy said with a grin as she looked at the women.

"What's that?" Megan asked, shaking her head.

"We have one dog and one beautiful kitty in the front who need a foster home. They have been shoved in a corner." Judy smiled and clapped her hands in front of her as she looked at Megan. "I noticed you aren't wearing a wedding ring. Do you live alone?"

Megan stuttered for a moment before she could reply. "Yes, but…."

"Don't you think having a nice doggy by your side would be comforting?" Judy gave her the brightest smile in anticipation.

Megan started to shake her head. "I don't know anything about pets. I've never had a pet."

"Really? Never ever?"

"No, Judy, never ever. I wouldn't know what to do," Megan said looking to Georgie for help. Her friend crossed her arms, cocked her head to the side and smiled.

"You know, Judy," Georgie said with an evil grin on her face. "I think a pet may be the perfect solution for Megan. She's been a tad lonely since her grandmother passed away and I think she could use some pet therapy now."

Megan scowled as she looked at her friend.

"Oh, that would be wonderful," Judy said. "And as the new leader of the Stanford Grant, you would offer a wonderful example by adopting a pet from the clinic."

"A temporary pet," Megan said, trying to back pedal.

"Of course, Dearie," Judy said. "Let me get things ready." Judy rushed into the clinic to ready two of the animals housed in the front room.

Megan glared at Georgie. "I can't believe you just hung me out to dry."

"Hey, my mother is fostering a dog. You have plenty of room in Misty Manor. You could probably fit fifty animals in there."

"Yeah, right. Thanks a lot."

Georgie laughed as she saw her friend start to fume.

"I'd better tell Nick we're done. I don't know if they need me here anymore."

"The car is open, right?" Georgie asked.

"Yes, as far as I know." Megan shouted behind her as she made her way inside the clinic to find Nick.

Twenty minutes later, Megan arrived at the car to find Georgie in the passenger seat and a large dog in the back. On the floor was a paper bag. Megan swung into the driver's side and looked at Georgie sideways. "Could you pick a bigger dog?"

Georgie laughed. "Meet Dudley. Dudley, this is your new mommy, Megan."

"Temporary hostess, that's it."

"What did Nick have to say?"

"Nothing more. He can't tell me anything about the investigation. Just that he'll be there for a while, so we should go home, and he'll call me when he can, which will probably be a couple days by the look of things." Megan huffed as she pulled away from the curb. "I guess Teddy will give them more information in the morning."

"Sounds good to me," Georgie said. "Let's get you settled and then I have to go home and help my mother with her new friend."

CHAPTER 6

*M*egan pulled the car as far as she could in the driveway and parked. She looked at her friend and continued to complain. "Seriously, Georgie. I don't know what to do with animals."

"For cryin' out loud, it's not that hard," Georgie said. "They're like children. You keep them warm, fed, and comfortable. Just remember, whatever food and fluids go in, eventually must come out, so give them plenty of opportunities to go to the bathroom."

"Hmmn, Georgie. Why do you keep saying them?" Megan leaned forward to get out of the car but stopped when her friend didn't answer. She looked back at Georgie who was watching her with pursed lips. "What? Oh no, what did you do?"

"I didn't do anything. Talk to your friend, Judy. Remember, you introduced her to me."

Megan turned around but didn't see anyone other than Dudley in the back seat. She looked back at Georgie. "What am I missing?"

Just then, she heard a small mew coming from the floor behind her seat. "What's that?"

"I believe it's a small cat," Georgie said with a wide grin. "Remember when Judy said there was a dog and a cat?"

"A cat? What the heck am I going to do with a cat and a big dog?

He must weigh 70 pounds," Megan said as she sized him up. She looked around the car. "Where the hell is the cat?"

"Dudley weighs 80 pounds to be exact and Judy told me to let you know he eats twice a day. He larger than most dogs of his breed."

"I don't believe this," Megan said, her frustration evident.

"The cat is in his carrier, which is in a paper bag on the floor," Georgie said as she shrugged. "Apparently, the cat loves bags, but to keep him safe they used a carrier in a bag."

"Really, Georgie?" Megan said, exasperation in her tone.

"Someone brought the cat to the clinic when his mother passed away a couple of weeks ago. Dudley had been there for a while, waiting for his forever home and was apparently somewhat depressed. When the cat came along, and his name is Smokey by the way, Dudley adopted the cat. He was instantly protective and happy again. Judy said there was no way she could separate the two."

Megan simply stared at Georgie.

"You can close your mouth now. Let's get your little pet family inside and set up for the night, shall we?"

Megan shook her head and got out of the car. She opened the back door, not knowing what to expect. Dudley simply looked at her, his big brown eyes imploring her for kindness.

"Oh, no you don't. None of that big, brown, mushy stuff, my friend. This is a short-term relationship."

Georgie shook her head on the other side of the car.

When Megan touched the leash, Dudley jumped up and out of the car but stopped and politely waited until his friend, Smokey, was addressed. Georgie came around, and picked up the paper bag with the cat carrier as well as a bag containing bowls, blankets and some toys. "Megan, there's a big bag of kibble and the dog bed in the trunk. Dudley can walk himself, so why don't you grab the food and I'll take the cat."

"Okay." Dudley watched from the side as she opened the trunk and brought out the bag of food. She lifted it and said, "Let's get this over with."

As they walked toward the house, Dudley veered off toward the ocean. He trotted toward the weeds on the side of the property.

"Hey," Megan yelled as she saw the dog run off. "The dog is running away." She dropped the big bag of dog food and began to run after Dudley.

"Megan, stop. According to Judy, Dudley is well trained. He's taking care of business before you go into the house."

Megan listened to her friend. She watched as Dudley nosed through the weeds for a few moments. He finally found a spot he liked and lifted his leg. As they waited, they heard another soft mew coming from the carrier. Dudley lifted his head and came running over to the group with a renewed purpose. He placed his nose close to the carrier and sniffed several times before whining. Smokey continued to mew and communicate with his trusted friend. Dudley then stepped back and looked up at Megan.

"What? Smokey's okay. If you're ready, let's go in and get settled."

The little party proceeded into Misty Manor and walked toward the kitchen. Georgie placed the carrier on the floor and then ran out to the car to get the remaining bags and dog bed. In the meantime, Megan folded a beautiful warm blanket and placed it in the corner of the kitchen for Dudley. She grabbed his bowls. Filling one with cool, crystal water, she placed it in the corner near the blanket. Dudley was grateful and lapped up the clear drink. Megan then poured some dry food into the other dish and placed it next to the water. Dudley sniffed but was not as interested in the dry food.

The dog was further distracted when Smokey continued to mew in the carrier. Megan realized the cat wanted to be free, but she waited until Georgie returned from the car with the rest of the supplies. Thinking it over, Megan was certain these were the first pets ever to set foot in Misty Manor. She knew there had been no pets while she was growing up and never heard her grandmother speak about any furry friends. Well, they were welcome to spend the night in the kitchen and maybe, if she was lucky, they could go back to the clinic tomorrow. Megan also made a note to remind herself to consider placing Georgie on the board for the animal clinic. Georgie seemed such a natural with the animals and Megan remembered she had owned a dog when they were in high school.

"We have a problem."

Megan looked up to see Georgie standing in the kitchen doorway, holding a big brown pan and something that looked like a scooper. "What now?"

"I have the pan for kitty, but we forgot to take litter."

"And that means?"

"It means Smokey will be using part of your home as a bathroom, instead of his litter box," Georgie said with a nod of her head. She walked into the kitchen and placed the pan on the floor.

"We can't have that," Megan said with wide eyes. "Now what?"

Georgie thought for a moment before turning to Megan. "Didn't I see a sand pail on the back porch?"

"Yes, I use it from time to time," Megan said with a laugh when she saw Georgie's face. "Don't judge me. We use sand for many things around the house."

Georgie laughed and pointed to the back door. "This will be one of those times. Go, get it."

Megan went out the back door and returned in record time with the sand pail and attached shovel.

Georgie led her to the front door. "C'mon, let's go." She turned to the two animals in the kitchen. "Stay right here. We'll be back in a few minutes."

The two went out the front door, across the porch, down the steps and walked toward the beach.

"What are we doing?" Megan asked.

"We're getting sand for Smokey's litter box," Georgie said.

"Okay, if you say so," Megan said as she followed along. She took a few deep breaths and looked up at the sky. "It's a beautiful night for December."

"It's been warm this Winter," Georgie agreed. "Nice full moon, too."

The two stopped at a level part of the beach and began to shovel sand into the pail. "I'm not used to this because we never had animals when I was growing up," Megan said as she continued to fill the pail.

"I've had plenty of pets," Georgie said as she stood and walked to the water's edge. She kicked off her shoes and plunked her feet in the dark water. "We'll put the sand in Smokey's pan tonight. Just make sure you add some baking soda to stop any odors and tomorrow we can get kitty litter from the store."

"Okay," Megan said. "But they may be able to go back tomorrow, so we should check that first."

Georgie looked down at her friend and was glad it was dark, so Megan couldn't see her smile. It was obvious her friend knew nothing about fostering pets. "We'll cross that bridge when we get to it." Georgie leaned down and picked up the full pail of sand. "Let's go."

Megan took a moment to rinse her hands in the water as she gazed up at the full moon over the Atlantic Ocean. "It really is a beautiful night."

The two walked back to Misty Manor without realizing it would be the last peaceful night for a while.

CHAPTER 7

$\mathcal{N}$ ick stood at the nursing station and heard various beeps and alarms around him. He wasn't sure if there was a problem. The desk was deserted. He didn't see anyone running around the floor and there were no overhead announcements alerting a rapid response team to report to a specific room. Various monitors before him had wavering lines which he knew represented traces of heart rhythms for patients, but he had no idea what was normal and what was not. It was late, and the floor had the forced hush one heard late at night in the hospital.

After a moment, he saw one of the nurses returning to the station. She was surprised to see him standing at the counter as visiting hours had ended a while ago, but realized it was an official visit when she acknowledged he was in uniform.

"Can I help you, Officer Taylor?" The young nurse looked down at his badge to verify his name. Then offered a large shy smile as she watched his face.

"I'm hoping you can," he said, nodding toward the desk. "I'm here to check on a patient, Dr. Arnie Stokes. He came in earlier with a gunshot wound to the back?"

"The veterinarian?" She asked, as she searched the desk for the clipboard containing report.

"Assuming you have only one, that would be him," Nick said with a smile.

"Here we go," the nurse said as she held the clipboard and turned several pages. She read for a moment and looked back at Nick. "You're here on official business with the police department?"

"As official as it can get," Nick said as he pointed to his badge.

"No disrespect, but at times we've had friends show up in uniform, but not officially connected to the case. They ask for information, but we have to be sure to prevent HIPAA violations."

"I'm with the Misty Point Police Department and I'm here for an official update of this case," Nick said, annoyance creeping into his tone. "If this guy dies, we have a homicide on our hands."

"Okay, fine," she said as she nodded. "Dr. Stokes survived surgery, but he lost a lot of blood. The bullet was removed during surgery, but there was plenty of damage to the spine and spinal cord. He's still in recovery so you can't see him."

"But he's definitely going to live?"

"He should survive but I don't think they have any idea of how much function he'll recover once he awakens."

"Meaning?"

"They don't know how much paralysis will be permanent. He'll have a long road ahead of him either way."

"Will he be able to remember what happened?"

The nurse put down the clipboard and gave Nick the look she normally reserved for residents when they began their first year. "Look, it's too early to have any specific answers for you. First, we see how he does post-op. Next, we work on healing, recovery and rehab. We won't know his baseline until he wakes up. Sometimes, patients have other problems after surgery like blood clots or heart attacks. It's day by day at this point." When she finished, she cocked her head ever so slightly and smiled at Nick.

Nick didn't answer as he was trying to decide if he was satisfied with her answer. "Okay, I get all that, but I need to see him regardless of what state he's in. Can you tell me where recovery is?"

"Fine, I'll take you there. You can look through the observation window, but there's no way you're getting in the room, dressed like that."

Nick looked down at his uniform, covered by animal hair and black powder from the crime scene. "Deal, just show me where he is."

CHAPTER 8

Megan woke when the early morning light crept through her blinds. She tried to roll over, so her back was to the window, but came face to face with a heavy body and warm breath. She let out a yell and jumped up in bed, her heart hammering in her chest. She looked down to see Dudley stretched out on the bed beside her. His head was resting on her opposite pillow. He lifted his head, opened his eyes and looked up at her.

"What are you doing here? I left you in the kitchen." Megan looked down at the dog as if she were expecting him to answer her. He leaned forward and licked her forearm. It was then she noticed Smokey was snuggled against his chest. The young cat opened his eyes and blinked at her several times.

Megan shook her head and dropped back down on her pillow. She was now face to face with Dudley. "I don't know if I'm more upset with the fact you're in my bed or that you both crawled in here without me even knowing." Megan looked at the small cat, so tiny and frail. "And how did you get all the way up to my room? You look too tiny to climb two floors and jump up on my bed." In response, she got a small mew from the tiny creature.

Throwing back the covers, Megan sat up. "That's it, time to get up.

I'm going to make a call to Judy and see what the status is with the clinic." At first, Dudley's ears flew straight up, then fell back down as he dropped his head on the bed. "Ugh," Megan said in defeat as she stood up and pulled the covers down. "Okay, let's go."

After a moment, Dudley stood up, stretched and stepped off the bed. The tiny feline rolled over as he lost his canine pillow. Dudley stood at the side of the bed and ever so gently picked the cat up with his teeth and carried him out the door.

Megan headed toward the bathroom to clean up and get dressed for the day. When she arrived downstairs, she went into the kitchen and found both Dudley and Smokey waiting for her by their bowls. "Oh, the two of you look hungry." Dudley wagged his tail as if he understood every word she said. Megan bent to collect the bowls and placed them in the sink. After washing everything well, she filled the water bowl with water and put it back on the floor. Smokey took a few small laps and backed away when Dudley moved in for a drink. In the meantime, Megan filled both bowls with the proper food and placed them on the floor. She watched the two animals eat with gusto for a moment, then turned to start a fresh pot of coffee.

Once the coffee was made, she fixed herself scrambled eggs, bacon and a slice of toast. Megan ate her breakfast under the scrutiny of Dudley who watched carefully to make sure she didn't drop any food on the floor. As she raised the last bit of eggs toward her mouth, Dudley watched the fork with laser focus until she stopped midway. "Are you telling me you want some of this?"

Dudley continued to stare at the fork with raised brown eyes. Megan lifted the fork a bit higher as he watched. Drool began to form near his mouth. "Okay, fine. You're killing me." Megan slid the bit of egg off her fork and fed it to Dudley. He then smiled happily and wagged his tail as Megan placed the dishes in the sink and washed them. She picked up all the bowls and washed them too. She was wiping off the counter when Dudley let out a loud bark and stood with his hair on end. Megan jumped at the sudden noise and almost dropped the towel.

Dudley ran out of the kitchen and headed for the front door. He stood guard and continued to bark until Megan joined him. Before she could look outside, there was a loud knock. "Some ears you have," Megan said as she looked over at Dudley. She looked through the window and turned back to the dog. "And a good sense of character." Standing on the porch was her biggest thorn, Mayor Andrew Davenport.

Megan opened the door a couple of inches. "Can I help you?"

"Yes, Ms. Stanford. I want to have a word with you about the Hand in Paws Animal Clinic." Davenport began to push the door wide open and was surprised when Dudley jumped into the opening and growled. Davenport jumped back, "Whoa, do you have a leash on that dog?"

"No, actually I don't," Megan said as she secretly hid a smile. "You'd better step back and stay on the porch, for your own safety."

"You'd better have a license and shots for that animal." Davenport stood on the porch and pointed as Dudley continued to growl.

"I took him home last night as a favor to the Police Department," Megan said. "I don't know what you want, but you'd better say it quick and leave."

Davenport's face reddened to a deeper shade of purple. "I came to say that I don't know what type of environment you're perpetuating but I'm planning on making sure the Hand in Paws Animal Clinic is closed down by the end of this investigation."

Megan took a deep breath. "I don't know what's going on here. I haven't spent a lot of time in the clinic but I'm sure it provides a much-needed service to this town." Dudley then stuck his nose through the partially opened front door and growled. "I think you'd better go for your own safety, Mr. Davenport. If you have any further questions, please call my attorney."

Davenport scowled. "You haven't seen the last of me."

"That's unfortunate," Megan said as she closed the door. She turned and leaned against the wood while she gulped in air. Dudley sat and looked up at her with raised eyes until Megan leaned forward and scratched his head. "I've got to thank you for your help with the

Mayor. He's not a nice guy and I'm glad you didn't let him come inside the house. But if it's anyone beside him, we must be nice, okay?"

Dudley closed his eyes while she scratched his head. A few seconds later, his ears perked back up and he looked toward the door.

"Please, don't tell me he came back," Megan said out loud. She looked through the window and saw Nick heading toward the front porch stairs. Megan turned to Dudley. "Stay here a minute, I'll be right back." She opened the front door and slipped onto the porch.

"Hey, Nick, how are you?"

Nick smiled as he dashed up the front steps and grabbed Megan around the waist. After a strong hug from his built frame, his lips found hers for some morning delight. Breaking away, he said, "Good morning, how are you?"

"Pretty good now," Megan said with a large smile as she wrapped her arms around his neck. "But I just had a nasty visitor. Andrew Davenport was here threatening me about the clinic. He wants it closed down and says I'm perpetuating a bad environment."

"That's hysterical," Nick said. "Let's go inside and talk about it."

"Okay, but Dudley, the dog I'm fostering, is inside. He was fine last night, but growled and was barking at Davenport."

"Did you reward him?"

Megan laughed. "I haven't had time yet. You appeared minutes after he left. I'm surprised you didn't see Davenport leaving."

"He was probably parked in the driveway out back. I came in from the boardwalk."

"Just be careful when you go into the house. I'm not sure how Dudley will react."

"You've got it," Nick said with a large grin.

Megan slowly opened the front door and poked her head inside. When Dudley saw her, his tail started wagging at super speed. "Dudley, I have a friend coming in with me so be nice." Megan stepped into the foyer.

Dudley continued to watch the door as Nick stepped over the

threshold. Nick looked at the dog and said, "Hey, good boy." Dudley immediately jumped up, placed his paws on Nick's chest and started licking his face. Nick gave him a nice body hug and scratched him behind the ears. "Wow, what a great dog."

Megan smiled as she watched them. "He must like you a lot, because he looked like he was going to take Davenport's head off."

"That's because he has great taste," Nick said as he continued to scratch his head. "What breed is he?"

"I have no clue," Megan said. "I've never had a dog before, so I'm not very good at this. I think Georgie said he was a boxer. Let's go to the kitchen. I have a small cat in there and Dudley has been very protective of him."

"Okay, let's go," Nick said as he gently detached from Dudley. They all walked into the kitchen and noticed Smokey was in the dog bed near the blanket, playing with a small cat toy. Each time he pushed it to the side, a small bell rang. Dudley immediately went toward the bed, and settled near his side. Within seconds, Smokey nuzzled against his stomach and curled up beside him.

Megan went to the refrigerator as Nick pulled a chair out from under the kitchen table.

"Would you like something to drink?"

"Water would be great," Nick said as he stretched his shoulders backwards.

Megan came back to the table with a cold bottle of water and put it down in front of him. "You look tired."

"I am. I didn't get home until early morning."

"So, what's going on? Do you have any idea what happened last night?"

"The only thing we know for sure is Dr. Stokes was shot. There had to be some sort of scuffle because things were knocked about and we found blood all over the place. They're testing it now to see if they can get any information. I'll bet a dime they find two different blood types."

"How is Dr. Stokes?"

"I went to the hospital to check on him last night, but he was just out of surgery, so he was unconscious. From what they told me, they'll keep him out of it for a while, so he doesn't wake up and move right away. He had a neurosurgeon perform some fancy surgery and they don't want to take a chance he'll wake up and incur some deeper damage to his spinal cord. Since we have no idea what's going on, we're posting security outside his room until further notice."

Megan and Nick both turned when Dudley lifted his head and listened. "I don't hear anything, do you?" Megan asked Nick as she watched the dog get up and pad once again to the front door.

"No, but obviously he does. Good ears. Having a dog at Misty Manor may be a wonderful thing for you."

"Wait a minute, I'm just watching him until he can go back to the clinic," Megan said with a laugh. "I've never owned a pet. I don't really know what I'm doing."

They had walked halfway toward the front door when they heard a knock. Dudley stood at attention facing the door.

"Who's there?" Megan asked as she looked out the small pane of glass.

"Megan, it's Teddy. Open up."

"Okay," Megan said as she began to fumble with the knob. "I want you to know I have a large dog in here." Megan pulled the door slightly open and then watched Dudley.

Theodore Harrison Carter stood on the porch and looked inside at the large dog. "Is it safe to enter?"

Megan looked down at the dog. "Dudley, Teddy is my friend so be nice." Dudley leaned forward and sniffed Teddy's hand, then began to wag his tail. Megan looked up at Teddy. "Looks safe to me. C'mon inside. We were sitting in the kitchen."

Teddy crossed into the foyer.

"Please, let me take your coat," Megan said as they passed by a Cherrywood round table in the middle of the marble foyer. Ten feet behind it was the majestic grand staircase.

Teddy removed his tailored Burberry cashmere overcoat and

handed it to Megan to hang in the closet. Underneath he was wearing a charcoal gray Brunello Cucinelli suit and holding a leather briefcase. Behind Teddy's back, Megan made a face at Nick and said, "You know, maybe the three of us should go into the library to talk. We can sit at the writing table."

"Sounds like a great idea," Nick said. "I'll bring Dudley to the kitchen." He took a step and called the dog who hesitated for just a second before following Nick in the kitchen. To make him happy, Nick dug one of the dog treats out of Dudley's food box and placed it on the dog bed. The dog looked at Nick with large sad eyes. "C'mon, I'm not trying to trick you, but the man is wearing a two-thousand-dollar suit. We can't bring him in the kitchen. Stay here and keep an eye on Smokey for us. We'll be back as soon as we can."

Dudley eyed him for a second more, then ate the treat and nestled in his bed next to the cat, who curled up near Dudley's neck. Once they were settled, Nick joined Megan and Teddy in the library.

"Okay, the pets are settled," Nick said as he took a seat at the table.

Teddy raised his eyebrows and looked at Megan. "Pets?"

Megan shook her head as she frowned at Nick. "No, not really pets. I'm fostering them until the police decide the clinic is safe. They won't allow anyone in one of the rooms until the crime techs are done processing the area. We had to remove the animals who were caged in there, so we called several families and volunteers to foster them until the police are done."

"I see," Teddy said as he nodded. "It's simply odd, I don't have too many memories of pets inside Misty Manor."

"Does that mean there was a pet here at one time?" Megan asked. "I don't remember any growing up."

"There definitely hasn't been one here in the last thirty years, but before you were born, there may have been a dog, which lived here when your father was small."

"Really? I've never seen a photo or heard about it."

"I don't think Dean appreciated his canine companion, but I do remember Rose being somewhat fond of the creature."

"Wow, I never thought about my grandmother having a dog. Do you know what breed it was?"

"I believe it was a boxer as well, named Jack," Teddy said with a smile. "Beautiful creature. Obviously not loved by Dean and probably protected by Rose, but that's another story altogether." Teddy made a point to look at his Rolex. "Time is flying by so perhaps we should get started."

CHAPTER 9

*T*eddy looked at Nick as he said, "Officer Taylor, can you tell me what happened at the clinic last night?"

"Is this off the record?"

"Yes, I'm asking to see what we need to do to get this cleaned up as soon as possible."

"How about you tell me about the Hand in Paws clinic first?"

Teddy chuckled as he shifted in his seat. "Is this off the record?"

Nick nodded as he smiled. "For now, but I can't promise what Chief Davis will or won't do."

"Understood. The Hand in Paws Animal Clinic opened approximately five years ago. Dr. Arnie Stokes applied to the Stanford Grant for money to run a clinic. There are few veterinarians near the beach and we had an issue with feral cats and lost dogs. Those issues with animals in the town of Misty Point escalated after Hurricane Sandy. The board members all agreed it would be a positive move for the town, as well as the animals who were hungry or mistreated. Rose Stanford agreed to supply the money and helped with finding the location. Dr. Stokes has run the clinic since then. His budget was granted and reviewed on an annual basis by our accountant and was always found to be in order."

"Is that typical? To review the budget?" Nick asked as Megan looked on.

"Absolutely. The first year we extended a two-year grant assuming it would take some time to get things organized. Each year thereafter, we required an accountant to look at the books as well as reports of how many animals were treated, placed, or housed."

"What do you mean by housed?" Nick asked as he looked back and forth at Teddy and Megan.

"Hand in Paws is a no kill shelter. That was Rose's non-negotiable condition to supplying the grant. Animals were taken care of until they were adopted. Never put down." Teddy said with a slight smile. "She was very compassionate that way. A wonderful woman."

"Were there any problems with the books? Any strange complaints or issues?"

"It's interesting you ask that question. The grant was due to be discussed for approval. We've been waiting for Dr. Stokes to give us information, but he was late with his report for the first time. Normally, we review everything, and then ask him to report to the board in person for discussion. After I received some initial informa- tion, I went to visit him because there were a few irregularities in the report and I have to say he seemed more stressed than usual."

"What type of irregularities?" Megan asked, her stomach beginning to knot.

"Weird things," Teddy said. "He ordered more supplies than usual, and the animal count was off. I visited him to check the numbers because I wanted the board presentation to be pristine." Teddy paused. "Actually, Rose liked it that way. She always wanted to review things before they were officially presented or discussed so she wouldn't be caught off guard. Anyway, when I asked him, he said some of the dogs had disappeared."

"Disappeared how?" Nick asked shaking his head as he looked at Teddy.

"As in, they were there when he left for the day and the cage was empty when he arrived the next morning."

"That's strange," Megan said. "Could they have run off or someone gone in there? Who else had access to the clinic at night?"

Teddy looked puzzled. "Very few. Dr. Stokes had a key but wasn't allowed to copy it. The only other person who has a key in case of emergency is Judy Bowan." Teddy reached into the leather briefcase which sat on the table. He pulled out a file and opened it. After flipping through a few pages, he handed the file to Nick. "She's in charge of all the volunteers, but she was checked as if she were a full-time employee. No criminal record, excellent referral letters. There's never been a problem that I know of and she denied having any knowledge."

Nick read through the application and flipped the pages. "Can I keep this?"

"Of course. I made a copy in anticipation of the investigation. You may keep that, Officer Taylor."

"Great, thank you. Does anyone else have a key?"

"I have a key as well," Teddy acknowledged. "Just in case neither of them were around during an emergency, but I've never used it." He turned to Megan. "I will make sure you get a copy as well."

"Thank you," Megan said with a smile.

Nick nodded as he digested the information before him. "Thanks, this will help us."

"I've answered your questions. Now, can you please answer mine? What happened in the Hand in Paws clinic last night? As a representative of the board I have a responsibility to the clinic and to Dr. Stokes."

"It appears there was an invasion and Dr. Stokes was shot. He's in Coastal Community," Nick started.

"Is he okay? Did he say what happened?" Teddy asked, concern evident in his voice.

"He hasn't said anything. The doctors operated on him last night, but they won't know how successful they were until he heals and goes to therapy," Nick explained.

"I don't understand, he's not talking?"

"He's very sedated right now," Nick said. "They don't want him moving until the surgery has time to heal. We can't ask him anything until he wakes up and even then we have no idea if he'll be able to identify his attacker."

"That's horrible," Teddy said. "Do you have any idea if it was random?"

"No, not really, but we don't think so. There was a struggle. We found blood in quite a few places and we don't think it all belongs to Dr. Stokes."

"How badly do you think the other person was hurt?" Megan asked.

Nick paused. "No idea at this point, but I wouldn't discuss details if I did. As you know, we don't release every detail, so we can authenticate any information which comes to us from witnesses."

"I don't understand," Teddy said while shaking his head. "There's never been an issue with the clinic except for those few trivial things."

"Were you aware every camera in the clinic was damaged?" Nick asked as he watched Teddy's expression.

"No, I wasn't. But that explains why Dr. Stokes couldn't give us any information when the dogs disappeared. We asked about the surveillance camera and he told us there was no images because it happened at night and the clinic was too dark for the cameras to catch anything."

"Do you think it's possible he disabled his own cameras?" Nick glanced at Megan sideways as he proposed the question.

"I've never had any reason to suspect Dr. Stokes of any nefarious behavior," Teddy said as he drew himself up.

Megan leaned forward and broke into the conversation. "So, what's going to happen to the rest of the animals? How long until you're done?"

"We'd like to keep the site clear for at least a few more days. With the help of the other volunteers, Judy said she'll make sure the animals are fed and taken care of."

"What about the fostered animals? When can they go back?" Megan asked.

Teddy broke in to the conversation. "They're the lucky ones. I think they should stay put for now. As a matter of fact, we should try to foster the rest of the animals until we get things settled. It obvious Dr. Stokes won't be back for a long while, if at all, and without another veterinarian, we shouldn't leave the animals unattended."

"I think that's a good idea," Nick said, nodding his head in agreement.

"Do you think there could be more danger?" Megan asked, with eyebrows raised and eyes wide.

Nick reached out and covered her hand with his for reassurance. "Probably not, but we should keep it locked up just to be sure."

"I think we need to have an emergency board meeting. We'll have to look for a new veterinarian right away."

"What happens if we don't find one?" Megan asked in a soft voice.

"We'd have no choice but to close the clinic," Teddy said with a frown. "As a charity, it's a non-profit so there's no money to be made, but it's a necessary service for the town and the animals that are dropped off there. The next clinic is several towns over and it's not a pleasant place. At least we make sure all animals who are housed are immunized and given a microchip."

Nick sat up and asked. "Did the dogs who disappeared have a chip?"

"Apparently not," Teddy said. "We asked Dr. Stokes, but he said the dogs were already registered to the clinic before he got there. He had planned on making sure all of the animals were eventually chipped and logged, but I guess he didn't have a chance before the dogs disappeared."

Nick shook his head as he frowned. "Something doesn't add up here. We'll keep investigating and checking the clinic." He pushed his chair back and stood up. "I need to go see if Judy is taking care of those animals. I also want to make sure we don't have volunteers trampling evidence by going into the back room." Nick looked at his watch. "She promised she wouldn't enter until the police arrived this morning to monitor the activity, but I'd better check it out."

Megan and Teddy also stood and followed Nick to the front door.

Nick turned and placed a quick kiss on Megan's cheek. "I'll call you later. Take care of your new friends."

CHAPTER 10

*A*fter watching Nick run off the porch and down the stairs, Megan and Teddy retreated into the foyer. "Megan, please come back into the library with me."

"Sure," Megan said as she followed him into the room. As she walked toward the Cherrywood door which led into the library, she glanced toward the kitchen and saw Dudley peek his head out to check on her. She waved at the dog before she went inside.

Teddy reached the table, pulled out a chair and indicated Megan should sit. When she did as he asked, he pushed her chair in for her, circled to the other side and sat down.

"I've been waiting for an opportunity to talk to you," he began gently. "We're all mourning the loss of your grandmother, Rose, and I've been trying to give you space, but it may be time for you to start attending the board meetings for the various charities the Stanford Grant supports."

Megan clasped her hands on the table before her. "Teddy, I was thinking the same thing last night. I want to continue her philanthropy. I'm willing to go and I need to learn about every charity I'm responsible for, but as I've already told you, I have no experience in board rooms. What if I screw something up?"

Teddy smiled. "That won't happen because I'll be there to protect you and your grandmother's reputation and estate."

Megan smiled. "If you're willing to mentor me, I don't mind trying it."

Teddy cleared his throat before he said, "Well, there's one thing I wanted to talk to you about. Do you remember I said I had someone to help you with the meetings?"

"Yes, but please don't tell me you're thinking of retiring or something silly like that."

"I am, but not quite yet. However, I'm getting up in years and we need to prepare for someday."

Megan looked alarmed. "The only reason this works right now is because I trust you inherently. I've known you my whole life and grandmother trusted you."

Teddy smiled at her. "That's very kind of you, but I'm older than your father so I'll retire someday. In the meantime, I want you to meet someone very special to me. He's just a year older than you and he'll help me take care of you, for now. One day, he'll hopefully take my place as guardian of the Stanford estate."

"He sounds very mysterious," Megan said as she tilted her head toward the attorney.

"He's a wonderful young man, but of course I'm prejudiced," Teddy said as he beamed.

"Who is he?" Megan asked.

"Jonathan Brandon Carter," Teddy said as he looked at Megan and waited for her response.

"I don't understand. He's related to you?"

"Megan, I didn't think you would remember, but Jonathan is my son."

"Your son? Teddy, I didn't realize, I mean, I don't remember you having family," Megan stammered. "You never showed us photos."

Teddy laughed as he watched Megan squirm. "Do you remember a day, a very long time ago, when you had a visitor? A blonde boy when you were about ten years old? The two of you spent the day together while Rose and I had some legal business to review?"

Megan paused for a moment as a faint memory tickled her brain. "I remember someone, but it couldn't be him. We went swimming in the ocean and he was so excited by the water, as if he'd never seen an ocean before. Then it started raining and we spent the rest of the day up in the cupola, looking out the windows, watching the lightning."

Teddy smiled and nodded, pleased she had a memory of him.

Megan laughed out loud. "We were very excited because someone brought us hot chocolate and cookies to eat while we were up there."

"That boy is my son."

"I'm confused," Megan said, perplexed. "I often asked Rose about the boy, because I never saw him again and he didn't come back. If he had been your son, surely you would have brought him by the house more often."

Teddy's face clouded as he examined his hands on the table. "Well, that's a bit of a long story. My wife and I weren't getting along very well back then." He looked up at Megan. "We met in England, fell in love and decided to come to the US. She was a bit younger than me. We wanted to live near the ocean and I was so very lucky to meet Rose. She helped us get settled in New Jersey and made us feel welcome. After a while, our son, Jonathan came along. We were ecstatic, but then my wife didn't feel well many days. We went to many doctors and she had tests upon tests and one day they told us she had cancer." Teddy paused and took a deep breath. He continued after a moment. "She wanted to go back to England, to be with her family. We hoped we could find better news there, but …," Teddy stopped speaking and swallowed hard.

"I am so sorry," Megan said, tears in her eyes. "All these years, I had no idea."

"That day, the one you played with Jonathan, was during one of his trips to America. It was the happiest day for me and for just a moment, I could pretend I had a little family."

Megan felt her heart skip. "You were in love with my grandmother?"

Teddy chuckled as his face reddened. "I did love your grandmother, but not quite in that way. She was a very trusted friend. I would have spent more time with her, but things were very difficult with your father's moods back then."

"What happened to your son?"

"When his mother died, he decided to stay in England with his aunt. She was a twin, so it was almost like he was with his mother. But that made things more difficult for me and I couldn't live like that, so I decided to return to America. Rose was kind enough to welcome me back with open arms to manage her estate and continue to be friends. She was lonely after your grandfather disappeared and, as you know, your father was a handful. We both needed someone to talk to. It's important to know someone cares."

"I feel so bad," Megan said, tearing up as she watched him tell his story.

"Well, don't," Teddy said as he squeezed her hand. "I've spent years trying to convince Jonathan to come to America and he has finally moved across the pond."

"That's wonderful." Megan was happy to see joy dancing in Teddy's eyes.

"Oh, it's not his first time. He did come across to go to Princeton, but then went back to England after he graduated. He's an estate attorney like his father."

Megan shook her head. "Teddy, I am completely floored by this."

"I can't wait until you meet him again. Maybe we can all have dinner one day, soon. Anyway, he'll help guide you through these meetings and decisions. You'll be fine."

Megan smiled as she squeezed his hand. "Thank you, Teddy. I'm looking forward to having dinner and seeing him again."

"Glad to hear. I'll reach out and ask about his schedule. Maybe he'd like to come visit the beach." Teddy stood and pushed in his chair. "We have a lot to do, my dear. I'll go ahead and schedule an emergency meeting of the board for the Hand in Paws Animal Clinic. We'll need to make some rapid decisions about the animals. If we intend to keep the clinic open after the police investigation is done, we'll have to hire a new veterinarian. It can be short term employment at first and if it works out, and Dr. Stokes does not return, perhaps it will turn into a more permanent position. We'll cross that bridge when we come to it."

"Sounds like a plan," Megan said as she stood. They walked into the foyer, where Megan reached into the closet to retrieve his coat.

"Do you have any specific plans tomorrow afternoon?"

"No, nothing specific," Megan said. She shrugged her shoulders and looked around. "I'll just continue cleaning, I guess."

Teddy noticed the pile of household goods and looked at her with raised eyebrows. "What's going on with the house?"

"I'm clearing some of the common items and have an appraiser coming to look at them. Perhaps I'll get a good offer from an antique shop."

"Make sure you authenticate everything before you let it go. A few items may look old, but there may be original furniture or hand-crafted items that will have much more value than what you're offered," Teddy warned as he surveyed the pile.

"I will, I promise. You should also know that I've asked an architect to give me an estimate on work needed to repair and possibly restore Misty Manor."

"A splendid idea," Teddy agreed. "It would be nice to see Misty Manor in grand style once again and you certainly have the funds for it now."

"Thanks, Teddy. I've chosen someone who specializes in Grand Victorian homes."

"Excellent idea. Be sure to keep me updated and let me know if I can be of any help."

"I most certainly will," Megan said as she opened the front door. Teddy buttoned his coat. He passed by her and shook his head. "It's so difficult to live near the ocean during the Winter. The weather is so fickle. One never knows if they'll enjoy a warm day near the water or need protection from a cold, blustery wind."

"I'm hoping for the warm, sunny day in Winter." Megan looked toward the ocean and sniffed the air. She turned back toward Teddy and said, "You can't smell the beach in the Winter. It's not the same without the smell of the brine, grilled cheeseburgers, and sun tan lotion."

Teddy nodded. He walked to the top of the stairs, stopped and turned toward her. "Have a good day. I'll call you as soon as I've set up the emergency board meeting for the clinic." He then hurried off the stairs as he turned up the collar of his coat.

CHAPTER 11

*T*he volunteer watched as Judy stood at the front of the semi-circle and offered instructions to the group. The poor animals had to be fed and given their medication, but they wouldn't have as much fun today. They weren't allowed to leave their cages and play. All because the vet stuck his nose in where it didn't belong. The volunteer had no choice but to shoot him. He heard Dr. Stokes was still unconscious. Hopefully, he'd stay that way. Otherwise, things would get worse if he woke up.

The volunteer looked up as Judy called his name and gave him an assignment. He was happy with today's job. He liked the dogs he was given to care for, loving and fun to play with. Not like the older one in the corner. Maybe something would happen to that stupid dog, but he had to wait until he was told what to do. He didn't always like his assignment. Sometimes it was easy, sometimes it was not. Each week, he was given a special job and when he delivered, everyone was happy.

His job would be more difficult now, depending on what the police did. It was easier to steal things from the clinic and he hoped it wasn't shut down.

Before now, he lived in shelters and slept in a car. It had been harder to steal things or get money when he was homeless. But he may not be able to stay in the clinic now. Why did the veterinarian have to walk into the supply room? Things had been going well for months. Now, they had a big problem. Maybe he would help the animals today and ask questions after work. But he was always told to keep his opinions to himself.

The volunteer didn't really like what he had to do but he was stuck listening to orders. He could be jailed or worse if he talked. Maybe he should just listen and keep his mouth shut, for now.

CHAPTER 12

*M*egan closed the front door and turned toward the foyer. She looked down the hall and saw Dudley stick his head out the kitchen door. "It's okay, everyone's gone now."

Dudley walked toward her, his tail wagging and a smile on his face. *That's funny, she thought, do dogs smile? It sure looked like it.*

"Hi, how are you boy?" Megan bent forward and scratched the dog behind the ears. "I'll bet you have to go outside by now, don't you? Let me get the leash and we'll go for a little walk." As if he could understand her words, his pace quickened as he followed her to the kitchen. Megan found Smokey in the corner playing with a toy. He looked up when they walked in and watched them carefully. After a few moments, he went back to sniffing his toy.

Megan grabbed the leash while Dudley trotted to the front door. He stopped and turned to look back, his expression asking, what's taking so long? Megan finally reached him and bent forward to attach the leash to his collar. Turning the knob, she opened the door and Dudley eagerly pulled her onto the porch. She held the leash as she closed the door behind her. Dudley was panting and eager to start moving.

They made their way down the stairs, over the lawn and onto the grassy area before the beach. Dudley's nose was working overtime as he sniffed the grass and barked at the base of a bush. He looked up and watched several birds fly overhead. Excited, he jumped up as if he wanted to snatch them out of the air.

A few seagulls landed on the sand several feet away from the dog. He stood still and watched as they pecked the sand and turned their heads to the right and the left. Initially, nothing moved, then unexpectedly, Dudley took off. The leash was pulled from Megan's hands while she watched the dog run full speed toward the water. As he ran through the group of seagulls, they took off, shocked into flight by his sudden burst of speed. Stunned for a moment, Megan ran after him, calling his name. "Dudley, Dudley, stop!"

The dog turned and looked at her and then panted happily until she caught up. Megan bent to grab the leash and then scolded the dog. "Why did you do that?"

"Because he's been locked in a cage for who knows how long?"

Megan started at the voice. She looked up and shook her head. "Georgie, you scared the hell out of me."

"I'm sorry, but I was on my way over to see how you made out last night and I saw you running down the beach."

"Dudley wanted to go outside to do his business. He saw some birds and took off. He pulled the leash right out of my hands and I was afraid he would run away."

"Looks to me like he stopped when you called out to him," Georgie observed, leaning down to pet the dog.

"He did," Megan agreed reluctantly.

"Then I doubt he's going to run away. Megan, he's been locked in a cage for a while. For cry'n out loud, let him run."

Megan looked at her friend. "What if he doesn't come back?"

Georgie burst out laughing and pointed to the dog. "Look at him."

Dudley was sitting in front of them, watching them talk back and forth. Although Megan held the leash, he was not pulling or straining in any way. "Give the dog a break and let him run. There are no other people here and it's your private beach so no worries. Take the leash off."

Megan frowned but leaned down to follow Georgie's suggestion. "If you say so, you've had more experience with dogs than I have." She unclipped the leash and watched Dudley. He simply sat where he was and didn't move.

"Go, mush, run," Megan said, but he still sat there.

Georgie giggled and walked over to near-by brush. She rummaged for a minute or so and found a stick. She came back to Megan and handed it to her. "Here, use this. Throw it for him."

Megan did as she was instructed and took the stick. She threw it toward the ocean. Dudley took off, retrieved the stick and ran back to them with his prize in his mouth.

"Good boy," Megan said as she petted him. "You came back, what a good boy."

Dudley dropped the stick at her feet, backed up a step or two and wagged his tail in excitement. "You want me to throw it again?" She leaned down, picked up the stick and threw it as hard as she could. They were only a short distance from the water and the stick landed on top of a wave. Dudley raced to the water's edge, paused for a moment and then crashed into the ocean to retrieve the stick. He snatched it from the water and brought it back to them. As Megan leaned forward to pick it up, Dudley shook his whole body splattering her with chilly water.

"Oh, no," Megan yelled as she turned her face.

Georgie belly laughed as she watched her friend. "It's only ocean water, Megan. You'll survive."

Megan wiped her face with her sleeve. "Georgie, it's December at the Jersey Shore. That water's cold. He could have walked a few feet away before he did that, don't you think?"

"Next time, don't throw it in the water. It was cold for him, too." Georgie shook her head.

"I didn't throw it in the ocean on purpose," Megan protested.

"C'mon, let's walk toward the lighthouse," Georgie said. "Tell me what's going on with the investigation so far."

The girls turned and started walking to the Point.

"I don't know anything new. Nick was here this morning and

talked with Teddy. Either they don't have a lot of details or they're not sharing them if they do and Dr. Stokes is heavily sedated at the hospital, so we can't get any information from him. Teddy's calling for an emergency meeting of the clinic board of directors."

"Is the veterinarian going to make it?" Georgie asked.

"I think so," Megan said. "They're waiting to see how much damage was done to his spine. Hopefully, the surgery was successful and minimized complications."

"Maybe he'll wake up and be able to tell us exactly what happened."

"It's possible," Megan agreed. "But it's also possible he didn't see his attacker."

"He must have gotten a few hits in. Didn't I hear Nick say there was a lot of blood around that room last night?"

"Yeah, I heard that too. Maybe it didn't all belong to Dr. Stokes." The girls walked down the beach with Dudley running and trailing behind them. He would chase the seagulls then run back to their side. The dog appeared to be having the best day of his life.

Georgie bent forward and scratched Dudley behind the ears. "He's so happy being out of his cage. What a great dog."

"I'm sure he'll find a lovely forever home one day," Megan said with a shrug.

Georgie looked at her friend and decided not to reply. In the last six months, Megan had lost her job, her grandmother and had to battle her father over ownership of Misty Manor. Although pets may give her the love she so desperately needed, there was always the possibility Megan would feel burdened with their care. In the meantime, she and Amber would try to keep her spirits up. "Where's Nick now?"

"He was going to the clinic to recheck the crime scene and check on Judy."

"As the board chair, you could show up to get an update for the board meeting," Georgie suggested.

"That's true," Megan said, pursing her lips and tilting her head. "I forgot to tell you, our esteemed Mayor showed up here this morning issuing threats to close the clinic completely." Megan laughed. "He blamed me for this incident."

"He's an ass, but more reason for us to be on top of everything."

"I agree," Megan said as she looked at her watch. "The appraiser is not coming until later this afternoon, so we have some time."

"Okay, let's go as soon as we finish this walk."

"You got it," Megan said. She picked up the pace until they reached the Point. Megan stopped to take a breath and looked up at the lighthouse, hoping to catch a glimpse of Billy, the man who kept the lighthouse working.

"What are you looking for?" Georgie asked, looking up as well.

"I was thinking of Billy. I know Tommy helps him when he needs it, but I'm thinking I should check on him more often. He's getting up in age. He could easily fall and get hurt."

Georgie pulled her by the arm. "C'mon, let's get to the clinic. I'll call Amber and Tommy and make sure they check on Billy this afternoon."

"It's a deal," Megan said as the two women turned and started making their way back toward Misty Manor. Dudley walked beside them, darting back and forth toward the water. "By the way, where's Amber been? I haven't heard from her all week."

"I talked to her last night," Georgie said. "She was away for corporate training but she's back now."

"Did Tommy go with her?" Megan asked as she looked at her friend.

"I don't think so," Georgie said. "The two of them are becoming much closer, but these events are not something you bring your boyfriend to unless you get special permission. I'm pretty sure they're not at that point, yet. Plus, she was in a hurry to meet him last night."

"Was the band playing somewhere?"

Georgie shrugged. "No idea but I don't think so. I know Tommy and the Tides have a few gigs lined up for Christmas parties coming up around here, but I don't have details."

"Which parties?"

"Amber mentioned they were playing for some of the local companies. Some of these corporations have big galas."

"Interesting," Megan said as she nodded her head in thought. "I wonder if the Stanford Grants have anything scheduled. I should ask Teddy."

"I'm sure they do, and it may be high time for you to make an appearance and start meeting the people you'll be working with."

"That would be interesting," Megan said with a smile. "You never know where you can find information that would help solve a mystery."

"Well, you'd better ask him quick. This Saturday is the first weekend in December, so I'll bet there's a party somewhere."

Megan smiled as she turned to Georgie. "You know, I think I'll do just that." Once they reached the porch, Megan said, "Let's check on the cat and get my keys."

CHAPTER 13

As they drove up to the Hand in Paws Animal Clinic, they noticed a lot less activity on the street than the night before. Although there were several cars, Megan was able to park near the curb right in front of the building. After stepping out of the car, she opened the back door and withdrew the leash connected to Dudley's collar.

"C'mon, boy," Megan said as she led Dudley out of the car and across the grass. Georgie followed from the other side and they both approached the back door of the clinic. Pushing the door open, Megan called out as she peeked inside. "Hello?"

In front of her there was a flurry of activity. Crime techs were engaged in activities about the room. They wore gloves as well as special uniforms and carried boxes back and forth. Walls and floors were being scrutinized for bullet holes. Trace evidence was being collected.

Megan looked up and saw Nick. He was speaking to several officers in the back of the room, issuing instructions as he pointed to a wall with dried blood stains. After they walked away, Nick turned and saw Megan standing at the door with Georgie and the dog. He held up his index finger, indicating she should give him a minute to finish up business. Giving a final instruction, he walked across the room and met them with a smile. "What's up?"

For the first time in a long while, Megan fumbled for words as she reconsidered whether they were intruding where they shouldn't have been. "Sorry, Nick, I didn't mean to bother you. I spoke with Teddy for a while after you left, and I thought we would check on the status of the clinic."

"As you can see, we're still in the middle of collecting evidence," Nick said. "We sealed the room last night so no one could enter. Once the investigators start examining the evidence, they send us back to look for things that didn't seem pertinent the first time we were here."

Megan looked behind him and nodded her head. "That's pretty interesting. Have you found anything yet?"

"You never know until you get it back to the lab," Nick said. "What looks important to us may not be important at all and vice versa."

"So, what are you looking for today?"

Nick looked around before he spoke. "I'm really not allowed to say anything."

"Well, as the person in charge of the clinic, can't you let me know the status of the investigation?"

Nick frowned, then leaned toward the women before he whispered. "We got the bullet fragment that was removed from Dr. Stoke's spine. Now we're checking the walls and other areas to collect any other bullets. It's very different in the daylight. That's why we seal the crime scene and come back to recheck."

"Did you find anything?" Megan asked, looking up at Nick, worry etched on her forehead.

"Nothing," Nick said as he pursed his lips. "And that's the point. We also didn't find a gun which means the shooter was well enough to run off with it."

"Good point," Georgie said watching the investigators over Nick's shoulder.

"We won't get prints off the primary bullet, now that it's gone through surgery, but we can see if there are any hits on it from other crimes. Maybe we can match something."

Megan frowned. "So, assuming there was a struggle of some kind, the shooter wasn't badly enough hurt to leave the gun."

"You got it," Nick said as he frowned.

"And we still don't know who all the blood belonged to or how the intruder was hurt?"

Georgie looked at her friend and laughed. "Any more deductions you want to make?"

"No, I'm just collecting facts," Megan said as she squinted at Georgie.

Megan turned to Nick. "Do you think this was a random shooting?"

Nick looked at the two girls, carefully considering how much information he wanted to discuss. "Don't start getting nervous about random violence. The clinic is in an out of the way area for a random shooting. Usually, there's something connected to a case like this, but we just haven't found it yet. We have to look at everyone connected to the clinic as well. That's why I'm still waiting for more information from your side, but other than that, stay out of it."

"Teddy's going to set up an emergency meeting to discuss the clinic. What are you looking for specifically?"

"Names, dates, incidents, records of disgruntled customers."

"Who are you concentrating on?" Megan asked, looking down at Dudley. He was sitting next to her, watching her speak with Nick.

Nick shrugged. "Everyone we can. Workers, volunteers, pet owners. Teddy mentioned there were a few irregularities in the budget, didn't he? I'd like to find out who's connected to those areas."

"Speaking of volunteers, did they all show up and take care of the pets today?" Georgie asked. "We came to ask if Judy needed any help."

"I don't know about that," Nick said as he turned and looked at the room behind him. "I know there are volunteers in the front room, but I have no idea if they all showed up. That's one reason why I need a list of the volunteers, so we can start checking them out."

Megan smiled as she looked up at Nick. "Well, we need to go talk to Judy about kitty litter. It looks like my furry friends will be spending a few more days with me."

Nick nodded and smiled back. "I'd appreciate it if you would go around to the front door. We don't want anyone walking through here."

"You've got it, Nick," Megan said with a half-smile." She turned and gestured to Georgie to follow her. Looking down at Dudley, he was up and ready to go, ears back and tail wagging.

CHAPTER 14

*R*ounding the building, Megan and Georgie reached the front door of the clinic. Dudley was right beside them and although Megan was holding the leash, there was no tension on it as Dudley stuck right by her side. They opened the door, and stepped inside the room.

The December ocean wind was chilly behind them but the air inside the clinic was warm and welcoming as they stepped inside. Megan placed her hand on Georgie's arm to stop her from going inside. She leaned over and whispered, "Start taking notes for Nick. Let's count how many people we see in here and report back."

In front of them, Judy was talking and directing a few people to feed certain animals, while others were changing water bowls or cleaning out cages. The girls counted eight volunteers, three men and five women following Judy's direction.

"Can I help you?" Judy walked over to the women when she saw them standing near the door.

"Hi, we came in to see how the animals were this morning," Megan said as she smiled at the volunteer director.

Judy clapped her hands together. "Dudley, how are you this morning, my precious baby?"

Dudley looked up at Judy, but didn't react. Megan smiled, "He seems to be fine, so far. I think he slept well last night, although he didn't have much time to get used to his foster home."

"Oh, you're the lady who's in charge of the grant," Judy said as she looked up and recognized Megan from the night before.

"Yes, that's right," Megan said sheepishly, realizing it was high time to own her position. "Maybe you can help me. I'm just learning about the grant. Could you tell me a bit about the clinic and the volunteers?"

Judy stood upright and turned to survey the room. "Yes, of course. I don't know much, but I'll be happy to share with you. I'll do every-thing I can to make sure the clinic stays open."

"Years ago, they started having a severe problem in Misty Point. The number of feral cats were increasing as well as stray dogs. Some renters would come for the summer, with their pets, and when the season was over, they would return home and leave their dogs here. The final straw was after Hurricane Sandy." Judy shook her head as she spoke. "Everyone was ordered to evacuate but you'd be amazed at how many families left their pets behind. Perhaps some people couldn't find their dog or cat before they ran out, but some didn't consider their pet important enough to take with them. Anyway, the town had a lovely gentleman who drove his truck around the streets for hours scooping up as many stray dogs and cats as he could find before the storm. He stayed as long as he could and then was forced to head inland when the storm hit."

"That's terrible," Georgie said as she looked around the room. She felt bad for the animals in their cages, but they were warm, dry and fed. "I mean about the owners, not the man."

"I don't want to think about the animals he didn't find," Megan said as she realized the implications.

Judy shook her head. "Yes, many animals were lost. Finding and making arrangements for them is one of the worst jobs after a disaster."

Mentally shaking herself off, Megan asked, "So, what happened next?"

Judy took a deep breath and continued. "Well, the shelters near the shore were full at the time. Luckily, we had offers from several people who owned large farms inland to foster the animals until the storm was over. Of course, months went by before owners and their pets were reunited. In some cases, their owners never came back."

"That is so sad," Megan said, tears forming in her eyes.

"Yes, it is," Judy agreed. "With the shelters being full, accommodations were taken wherever they could find them." Judy turned to Megan and gave her brightest smile. "But that is where your grandmother came shining through like a beacon of light in a dark cloud."

Megan turned to Judy and focused her attention on every word. "When Rose heard of the difficulties these poor animals were having, she located this building, which fortunately did not suffer any flooding. Dr. Stokes was looking for money and agreed to run the clinic. Rose purchased the cages and runs that were necessary and funded the shelter, so the animals were able to have a place to go and be cared for. Her number one condition was that all pets be loved until they found a forever home. No animal could be euthanized simply to make room or because time had run out."

Megan swallowed hard and realized tears were running down her cheeks. She wasn't sure her emotions were about the animals as much as the fact she missed her grandmother more than anything at that moment. Megan also wished she knew her grandmother better, now that she was an adult. As a child, you instinctively love your family but never see them the same way other people do or appreciate their values and generosity.

"I'm sorry, I didn't mean to upset you," Judy said as she pulled a small packet of tissues out of her volunteer smock.

"That's okay," Megan said with a sniff. "Grandma Rose's death is still a little raw for me, that's all."

Georgie stepped up with a bright voice, "Judy, we stopped in to see how you were doing but while we're here, we need to pick up some kitty litter."

"Oh, we have some in the corner," Judy said as she pointed to the side of the room. "We may be a bit low ourselves. I'll have to check."

"Don't worry about it," Georgie said. "We can pick some up on the way home from one of the local stores. I don't want to take any if your supply is low."

"Why, thank you. That's an issue I haven't thought of. How are we going to get supplies?" Judy turned to Megan. "Maybe you can consider that for me? Or if you give me permission, I'd be happy to do the ordering for you."

"I don't have any information for you, but I'll talk to Teddy and we'll make arrangements right away. It would be helpful if you could make a list of what you think you'll need."

"I'll start on that right away," Judy said, dimples popping out.

Megan's phone began chiming from her jacket. After looking at the number, she shook her head and said, "Never fails, if you talk about someone, they'll suddenly call you."

Megan pushed the green button and began speaking. "Hello? Teddy, we were just talking about you." She listened for several moments as the masculine voice on the other side of the phone spouted out information. "Okay, that sounds great. I'll be there." Megan clicked off her cell phone and stuck it in her back pocket.

"What was that all about?" Georgie asked.

"Teddy called to say he set up the emergency meeting for tonight," Megan said as she turned toward Judy. "Maybe we'll get some answers then."

"If you talk about the budget, please remember us," Judy said as she gestured toward the room full of volunteers and animals while making a boo boo face.

CHAPTER 15

*M*egan walked up the front porch stairs with Dudley leading the way. Closing the car door with her foot, Georgie followed behind carrying a heavy box of kitty litter. She caught up just as Megan unlocked the door and Dudley ran inside. Megan let go of the leash, so she wouldn't be pulled down as she walked into the foyer. She placed her purse and keys on a small table to the side of the front door and helped Georgie come inside.

"Thanks for helping me buy this," Megan said as they went into the wash room and grabbed the kitty box. "I had no idea what to get for the cat."

"First of all, his name is Smokey," Georgie said. When Megan turned to look at her, Georgie shrugged her shoulders. "What? I read the papers from the clinic."

The women walked out the back door, cleaned out the dirty sand from the box and washed it thoroughly. After drying it off, they went back into the wash room and Georgie helped to pour the clean litter into the pan while Smokey and Dudley watched with approval. "You'll get used to scooping daily."

"Can't wait," Megan said with a frown as she detached Dudley's leash from his collar. Both the women and animals turned their heads when they heard a noise at the front door. Dudley ran out to the foyer and gave a warning "woof" as Megan followed behind. She looked through the small window and saw Amber on the front porch with Tommy standing beside her.

"Hey," Megan said as she swung the door wide open and looked at the dog. "Dudley, these are my friends so be nice." Dudley wagged his tail and looked at the newcomers.

"Oh wow, I didn't know you got a dog. He's the cutest," Amber said as she rushed into the foyer.

"I didn't get a dog," Megan said. "I'm fostering a few of the animals from the clinic until they figure out what they're going to do with them."

"That's really nice of you," Amber said as she looked at Tommy. "Someone else has been thinking about getting a dog."

"I miss having a dog, but I'm not home enough to raise one. It's wouldn't be fair to the dog," Tommy said with a shrug.

"Aww, maybe someday," Megan said with a smile. "How are you two doing? Tommy, how's your Uncle Billy?"

"He's doing well, but his arthritis is acting up. It's December and the lighthouse is drafty."

"I know, and I feel bad about that," Megan said. "I've asked him, but he doesn't want to move out."

"Are you kidding me?" Tommy said. "He's lived there his whole life and will stay there as long as possible."

"Rose promised him he could, so that's his choice as long as it's safe for him," Megan said. "Maybe we can renovate the apartment inside. I'll have to check into that for him."

"That would be very kind of you," Tommy said as he petted Dudley's head.

"So, what else is going on?" Amber asked as she pushed further into the foyer. "I haven't seen you in a while. Suddenly, I'm hearing stories about a shooting and of course your name came up in the discussion, again."

"That's great," Megan said with a sarcastic smile. "More rumors around town about me. It's a good thing I moved back to Misty Point, otherwise the people in this town wouldn't have anyone to talk about."

Laughing, Amber and Tommy waved hi as Georgie walked out of the kitchen. "I guess no one told her we used to talk about her even before she moved back," Georgie said.

"Very funny." Megan placed her hands on her hips. Sensing her shift in mood, Dudley leaned against her leg. Megan reached down and stroked the big dog's head until he calmed.

"Back to rumors, I heard there was a shooting and that you own the clinic and it was one of your enemies from Detroit who followed you to New Jersey to get back at you," Amber said breathlessly.

Megan didn't respond for a moment then let out a hearty laugh. "C'mon, you're teasing me now, right?"

Amber paused, "Umm, actually no, I really heard that."

"Well, the rumor mill is working overtime. That sounds cheesy even for a book."

"Then what's going on? Enlighten us," Amber said as she pointed to herself and Tommy.

"I don't know anything except that Dr. Stokes, the veterinarian at the Hand in Paws clinic was shot last night. I have no idea why, or whom," Megan said.

"And how are you involved?"

"Grandma Rose initially funded the clinic through a Stanford Grant. Now that she's gone, the responsibilities for her charities have fallen to her estate, which she left to me, so now I'm involved."

"Wow, that's awesome," Amber said.

"What? The man was shot," Georgie said, shaking her head at her friend.

"Well, that wasn't good for him, but it's awesome Megan will be involved with all these charities."

"I'm glad to hear you say that because I plan to bring all my friends on board with me, so get ready for some meetings," Megan said cheerfully.

"That's interesting," Amber said. "My corporation does all sort of philanthropic things. As a matter of fact, they'll donate money to a charity of our choice once we've volunteered a certain number of hours."

"That's cool," Tommy said as he turned to Megan. "Hey, if you ever need a band at a fundraiser, Tommy and the Tides are at your service."

"Thanks, Tommy, I appreciate it," Megan said with a smile.

"I think that's a great idea," Amber said excitedly. "Let's have a fundraiser for the animals. It's December so we could call it the Holly Berry Craft fair or Mistletoe Magic."

Georgie smiled and pointed to Megan. "You're never going to believe this, but Megan is considering pulling the vintage Christmas decorations out of the attic and putting them up this year."

"Really?" Amber asked. "We could have our Ocean Holiday Walk and end up in the town square for a tree lighting. We haven't done that for years." Amber turned to Tommy and placed her hand on his upper arm. "That's where you and the guys can set up the band. We'll sell cookies, pastries and hot chocolate and collect donations for the clinic."

"Don't forget Santa handing out candy canes for the kids," Georgie said as she laughed.

Megan looked back and forth at her friends and realized how much she had missed being near them when she lived in Detroit.

"What?" Georgie asked as she watched Megan smile.

Megan shook her head. "Nothing, I was just thinking how lucky I am I have you as friends."

"Oh Lord, do you have any beer?" Georgie asked as the group surrounded Megan and pushed her toward the kitchen.

"I do," Megan said as they followed her and sat at the table. She pulled several cold, long neck bottles from the refrigerator, popped off the tops and handed them to her friends. They sat and talked about their idea while they drank the cold beer and enjoyed each other's company.

Megan looked toward the animals and noticed Dudley pick up his ears and run to the kitchen door again. "What's up, boy? You're better than a doorbell." The dog looked at her and woofed. Megan followed him to the front door once again. When she looked through the small window, she saw a middle-aged man, wearing a black overcoat and hat, standing on the porch.

Opening the front door a few inches, she asked, "Can I help you?"

"Hello, my name is Irwin Perry," the man said as he removed his hat and held it in his hands. "I have an appointment with Megan Stanford."

"Oh, yes," Megan said as she pulled the door wide open. "Please come in. You're the antiques dealer."

"Yes, I do specialize in antiquities," Irwin said as he entered the foyer, cautiously watching Dudley's response. The dog seemed to be waiting to decide whether he accepted Irwin as an approved guest.

Megan looked down and noticed the dog's behavior. "Please, let's go into the library so we can talk," she said as she showed him to the library door. "I'm going to bring the dog to the kitchen. Please have a seat and I'll be back in a moment."

Leaving Mr. Perry in the library, Megan walked out of the room and motioned for Dudley to follow her down the hall toward the kitchen. When she entered her friends looked up.

"Who was it?" Amber asked as she stood and started collecting empty beer bottles.

"It's the antiques dealer. Listen, I'm going to speak to him in the library. Can you guys wait for me?"

Georgie shook her head. "Sorry, I've got some things to do, so I'm going to run."

"Us too," Amber said pointing to herself and Tommy.

"Oh, okay," Megan said. "Let me walk you to the door, but I'm really glad you all came over."

"Hey, let's make a date to go to the Clamshell soon. Everyone needs to relax," Amber said. "I haven't had a chance to see you guys in weeks."

"I know, we were just talking about that," Megan said as the group left the kitchen. She watched them leave the house and walk down the front steps. The wind was still chilly. The waves were large, the birds were restless, and Megan felt unsettled, but she wasn't sure why.

CHAPTER 16

Megan turned and motioned for Dudley to behave as she walked into the library to join Mr. Perry. He was across the room, with his back turned to her, examining the shelves of books. He turned when he heard her enter the library. "Miss Stanford, you have a wonderful array of books here."

"Thank you," Megan said as she walked over to the bookcases. "They've been in my family for a long time."

"That's quite apparent. I hope you've invited me to look over your collection. I believe I saw several first editions of some famous classic books."

Megan was embarrassed to admit she had no clue what books were in the library. Grandma Rose loved the library and spent many contented hours there. Megan had a dim memory of her grandmother telling her the books were originally collected by her great grandparents. Some of the books were collections her great-grandfather, John Stanford, had carried home with him on one of his many voyages as a sea captain. Megan never really thought of the books as more than decoration, but made a flash decision to dedicate her time to catalog every title and edition in this room.

Grandma Rose enjoyed classic tales and Megan remembered

having books read aloud to her as a child. Grandma Rose choose books such as Black Beauty by Anna Sewell, Charlotte's Web by E.B. White, and The Secret Garden by Frances Hodgson Burnett. She wondered if those books were first editions.

When reading on her own, Megan loved to go into the cupola and read all day especially when it was raining at the beach. She would watch the rain, read a chapter and occasionally fall asleep from the peaceful atmosphere.

"Mr. Perry, I asked you here today to talk about some of the items in the house, but the books were not included in the things I put aside."

"That's a shame," Mr. Perry said as he looked up toward the ceiling. "From the looks of the library alone, there must be a great many treasures in this house."

"I suppose that would depend on what you consider treasure," Megan replied, tilting her head as she looked at the man. He was middle aged, with gray peppered short hair. He was wearing a modest dark suit, one of which could be purchased in any department store. His blue tie was silk and complemented the ensemble.

"That's an interesting comment coming from one who is so young," Mr. Perry said as he smiled and nodded. "How can I be of help?"

Megan paused while she thought of the proper reply. "As you know, my grandmother, Rose Stanford, passed away several months ago. I have been made the executor of her will, which is being handled by my attorney, Theodore Harrison Carter."

Mr. Perry smiled and nodded while she spoke. "Yes, I know him well."

"In her waning years, Grandma Rose was not able to maintain Misty Manor the way she used to. I've been thinking of sorting through the things she has here and restoring the house to the beauty of yesteryear."

"That's a very admirable goal," Mr. Perry said as he gauged her sincerity regarding the love of her house versus a sale to make a quick buck.

"I'm just not sure how to go about it," Megan confessed. "Part of me doesn't want to lose any of her memories but areas of the house need to be cleaned up."

Mr. Perry looked at her and then gestured to the table. "Why don't we sit and have a little chat?"

The two walked over to the table and made themselves comfortable. Mr. Perry still had a book in his hand which turned out to be a copy of Sense and Sensibility by Jane Austen. He smiled at Megan and said, "I think the first thing you need to do is examine your goals, for yourself and for Misty Manor." Looking around he added, "I'm not sure you even realize what you have here. Just this library alone, with its grand furniture and these books are probably worth quite a bit of money, if that was your goal."

Megan reddened and sat up straight. "I assure you that is not my goal. Misty Manor is to be cherished and restored. It will stay in my family, hopefully for generations to come, including all the treasures and memories that go with it."

Mr. Perry relaxed against his chair and smiled. "I'm very happy to hear you say that. I knew and admired your grandmother. She was a wonderful woman and I'm happy you're intent on preserving her legacy."

Megan visibly relaxed and said, "Thank you for saying that. I was very close to my grandmother."

"In order to advise you properly, I would have to ask you some questions about the history of your family and Misty Manor. Would you be able to give me those details?"

"Of course," Megan said, although now doubting herself, realizing she had less command of her grandmother's interests and possessions than she thought. "What would you like to know?"

"Let's start with the history of the house and the land."

"Misty Manor was built in the early nineteen hundreds by my great-grandparents, John and Mary Stanford. John was a sea captain who had been given a large parcel of land on the Jersey Shore. As a gift to his wife, Mary, he built a beautiful Grand Victorian and named it Misty Manor. The house was made of the finest materials, some of which were brought back from his travels to Europe. They lived here and raised their son, George, who was my grandfather. During that time, they also built a small town on the land and named it Misty Point. The lighthouse was part of the property as well."

"George grew up, was schooled at college and married a beautiful woman named Rose, my grandmother. They had a child in the 1950s and named him Dean. When my father was about five years old, George went missing. Rose was a resourceful woman and choose to stay at Misty Manor, always hopeful George would return to his home." At this, Megan looked up to gauge Mr. Perry's reaction.

"Go on," Mr. Perry said nodding his head.

"When John and Mary passed away, they willed the house to Rose, so she would have a place to raise my father, Dean. It's sad, she was always convinced George would return to her one day."

"I understand the mystery of his whereabouts were finally solved."

"As sad and tragic as it is, yes it was. I think Grandma Rose would have held on forever to make sure she found her beloved George before she died," Megan said, swallowing hard at the memory of her first month back home.

"I'm sorry moving back to New Jersey has been so painful for you," Mr. Perry said.

"Thank you," Megan said as she nodded.

"Please continue, if you feel up to it. I'd like to hear more about Misty Manor and the town."

"Yes," Megan said as she nodded. "I grew up in this house but honestly feel like I know little about it. It was very special to Grandma Rose. She spent a lot of time preserving and caring for Misty Manor and the items in it." Megan paused for a moment to compose herself, then turned back to Mr. Perry once again. "My goal is to restore Misty Manor to its former self, to fix damage from the storm, but also to learn more about my heritage. I want to know more about my great grandparents as well as my grandparents. I believe there's some very interesting history hidden in these walls, but I need a place to start and someone to trust who will guide me."

Mr. Perry smiled as he watched Megan speak. He realized she

looked and acted more like her grandmother than she realized. Her thoughts and plans were well placed, and he'd be happy to help her. "Megan, can I call you Megan?"

"Please do," she said as she watched him.

"Allow me a few moments to review antique collections and inheritances with you."

"That would be great," Megan said, feeling as if they were finally getting somewhere.

"When you inherit a home, or an estate, there are many things you can do with those possessions. For common value items, you may simply want to have a yard and garage sale or a larger estate sale. That decision depends on whether you are planning to keep the home or simply divest yourself of all the items. Other options include bringing items to a consignment shop, an auction or placing them for sale on an on-line shopping site. Collectors love to roam through estate sales because the person running the sale very often doesn't realize the value of some of the items they are giving away. A collector won't point out that you're selling a vase with a three-thousand-dollar value for two dollars. The older the home, the better the prospects."

Megan listened with interest. "I was asked if I wanted to have an estate sale, but to be honest, I didn't want a lot of nosey people raking through my things and I've heard items are commonly stolen as well."

"That's very true," Mr. Perry said. "That's the reason why you may want to hire a company to run a truly proper estate sale, but it all depends on the value of the items you have to sell. If you know the house contains expensive treasures and you decide to part with them, you could arrange a private sale to a collector or a museum. I've also been involved with some very high-end art and antique sales. For those types of sales, which can range into the millions, there's always a broker fee and private arrangements. Very often, there may be a bidding war from various collectors."

"What type of items are you talking about?" Megan asked, now more confused than ever.

"Antique items are varied. Valuable items can be furniture, windows, maps or rare books," Mr. Perry said as he pointed toward the bookcases. "As a sea captain, your great grandfather may have some very valuable early maps stored here somewhere. Collectors will also look for clocks, glass, rugs or tapestries. Don't even get me started on antique jewelry or ceramics. Some collectors only concentrate on china and crystal. Art and paintings are a category by themselves. Some very specific treasures have been hidden in attics or homes with no realization of their value or importance to society. Every artist or writer had to start somewhere before they were successful. Imagine if you found an early work by a renowned painter or an initial manuscript from a fabulous writer." Mr. Perry paused and smiled before he continued. "Every famous person had a mother or father or grandmother," he said as he smiled at Megan, "who holds on to their children's work, simply because of the emotional worth of that precious child, never dreaming of the monetary value or social worth that item may have one day in the future. To some, the most important value may be a beautiful gift crafted by their baby. You would be amazed to find how many people would purchase a macaroni necklace made by a famous person."

Megan didn't know whether to laugh or cry. She had made several macaroni necklaces for her family in school and had no idea if anyone ever kept them. "I have to admit I'm more confused than ever. I put aside a pile of things that my friend and I collected from some of the rooms upstairs. I have no idea what their worth or value would be, but my goal is not to raise money. I would like to keep the items that have historical value, or sentimental value and get rid of common items that clutter the home. I also need to have some areas contain the modern amenities for current living."

Mr. Perry crossed his legs at the knee and smiled at Megan. "Do you mind if I give you some advice?"

"Please do," Megan said as her lips trembled.

"Honestly, as an appraiser and collector, I've dreamt about looking in the rooms and hiding places in this home for a long time, but I've known your grandmother and Teddy and consider them decent, respectful people who have always helped others. I'm very sure I could bamboozle you out of many valuable items, but I won't do that out of respect for their friendship, but I'm certain other collectors wouldn't give it a moment's thought."

"Thank you for being honest," Megan said as she realized the vulnerable position she was in.

"Why don't we arrange a small meeting with Teddy and discuss our goals more thoroughly," Mr. Perry suggested. "I also want both of you to feel comfortable with any recommendations I make. Also, for you to only choose items you want me to see."

"That sounds like a great idea," Megan said, relieved at having an opportunity to rethink her plans. "I'll be seeing him later today and will discuss it with him."

"In the meantime, I'll take a quick look at the pile you put to the side and give you my thoughts on those items."

"Thank you," Megan said as she reached out to shake Mr. Perry's hand. "I think we'll have a lot to discuss."

CHAPTER 17

$\mathcal{T}$he volunteer walked through the back door, into the kitchen and dropped into a chair. He looked up when his boss walked into the room and cringed when he noticed his scowl. In practiced defense, he held his hands up and said, "Micky, it wasn't my fault. He saw my face. What was I supposed to do?"

Micky didn't say anything. He stood with his hands in his pockets, his tongue pressed against the inside of his cheek as he breathed through his nose. Finally, he walked behind the volunteer and slapped his ear with the back of his hand. "Jared, are you really that stupid?"

Jared jumped, leaned forward and grabbed the side of his head as he howled in pain. "Watch it, that's where the vet jabbed me with the scalpel."

"You deserve whatever pain you get," Micky screamed at the top of his lungs. "What were you doing there at that time of night?"

"Usually there's no one else there. I didn't expect the guy to walk in on me. Then he saw the things in my hands and he knew. He figured out it was me stealing all those things, so I had no choice."

"Except you didn't get the job done."

"What do you want from me? I had a scalpel shoved in my neck. I was in pain and bleeding. Look at this," Jared said as he pulled back the bandage on his neck. The exposed wound was red, swollen and had brown, green junk oozing out of it.

"That's disgusting," Micky yelled as he looked away from the wound. "And you went to the clinic today?"

"Absolutely, it would look suspicious if I didn't show up."

"Why didn't you put a sign on your back with a big arrow on it?"

Jared reddened while he listened to Micky, but kept still despite feeling the usual hatred for him. His fists clenched under the table near his leg. "It's December so I wore a scarf, wrapped around my neck all day."

"You realize you've put this whole operation at risk? I've already gotten a couple of calls about you. You've upset some people and they're not the kind I would want mad at me. I wouldn't turn my back on anyone if I were you."

Jared clenched his jaw but remained silent.

"This veterinarian recognized you?"

"Yes, he did."

"And what makes you so sure he didn't give your name to the cops?"

"He's still in a coma, according to the volunteers at the clinic today. He may never come out."

"You better hope he never comes out of it," Mickey said as he worked his jaw. "Go pay him a visit at Coastal Community but don't see any of the doctors there for yourself. They're probably on the lookout for someone with a neck wound."

"I've got to do something," Jared whined. "It hurts like hell and now I have a fever."

"Then go out of town for antibiotics," Micky said as he scowled. "Next time, don't screw up or you won't be needing any medications."

CHAPTER 18

Megan and Mr. Perry spent an hour looking over the pile of items she had put aside to be assessed. After determining they were common household things, Mr. Perry expressed a lot of interest in the Persian rug upon which they sat but Megan assured him she was not ready to part with anything from the house except for the pile which sat before them.

Mr. Perry told her he would make arrangements with a local dealer to pick up her items and include them in his next lot sale. The pair made an appointment to meet again. Together, they would create an inventory of the contents of the house. Megan would have a better idea of the value of her new possessions which would allow her to properly protect and obtain the necessary insurance.

Megan walked Mr. Perry to the door and watched as he left the porch and turned toward his car. She closed the front door and found Dudley and Smokey behind her.

"What are you two up to?" Megan asked as she spied them in the hall. Dudley's ears went straight up while Smokey rubbed up against Dudley's back leg. Megan smiled when she noticed they were so happy together.

Looking at her watch, she realized they must be getting hungry and she wanted to make sure they were fed before she had to leave for her meeting with Teddy and the rest of the board members for the Hand in Paws Animal Clinic.

The animals followed her into the kitchen and happily waited while she filled their bowls with fresh food and water. Dudley's tail wagged as he watched her work. Smokey kept rubbing up against her ankles. Megan stopped and looked down at the cat. She never owned one and never had a cat rub up against her before this moment. She leaned down to pet their heads and was rewarded with a big lick on the face from Dudley and purring from Smokey. "You two seem really cute, it's a shame I wouldn't be a good pet owner, but I'm sure you'll have a great new owner soon."

The animals continued to look at her as she placed their bowls on the floor. They eagerly dug in to their meals and drank the water. Megan waited until they were done so she could take Dudley outside to relieve himself. She picked up the leash but then thought about Georgie's comments about this part of the beach being private land, so she held onto the leash but opened the door to let Dudley run free.

Within seconds, he dashed out the door, down the steps and onto the lawn. He ambled over to a patch of grass and took care of business. He then nosed through the weeds for a few moments more and made a half-hearted attempt to chase a few seagulls as Megan waited and watched. Dudley realized there was not going to be a long beach walk so he didn't stray far and eagerly followed Megan up the porch steps into the house.

Megan walked him to the kitchen and placed the leash over the back of a kitchen chair. She picked up her purse and said, "Well, I'm glad the two of you enjoyed your dinner. I have to go to a meeting. I'll leave the light on in the kitchen and I'll try to be back as soon as I can, but promise me you'll behave."

Dudley looked at her for a moment, then curled up in the dog bed on the floor as Smokey climbed in and spread out next to him, taking time to lick his fur clean.

Megan left the house mumbling to herself. "I don't know why I feel guilty I'm going out and leaving the animals alone. That's why pets wouldn't work for me." She shook her head as she locked the front door and made her way to her car.

CHAPTER 19

*P*lacing the car in park, Megan turned off the engine and looked at the Misty Point Library. She spent many a day in a smaller version of the library when she was a young girl. The building was a brick structure several blocks away from the ocean on a pretty road full of trees and lawn. Thankfully, the location and the fact the building was made of brick ensured the structure avoided damage and flooding when the storm hit town.

Years ago, when town funds were scarce for projects such as upgrading the structure, money was privately donated to have the building reconstructed and shelves freshened with recent titles.

The library was becoming increasingly important in a beach town. The book stores which commonly sold beach reads were disappearing. Summer residents were obtaining library cards and using the facilities for the four months they summered at the shore. Megan realized how important it was to keep the content current and was happy someone donated money to keep it that way, but never realized it was her grandmother until Teddy gave her a brief rundown of her grandmother's charities and interests.

Megan wanted to keep all literary interests alive and for the first time missed being an investigative reporter. When she had a free moment, she wanted to spend time seeing what newspapers and periodicals they stocked as well as their current inventory of books, digital devices and computers. Public libraries were so much more than stacks of books in the current day and she would do her best to keep her grandmother's dream of helping the townspeople alive.

Years had gone by since Hurricane Sandy hit and there were still residents of the Jersey Shore who didn't have their homes rebuilt or connections to the internet. The library provided the needed support when they came into town to check on construction or progress of their claim. Megan made a mental note to talk to Teddy about the next library meeting. She wanted to attend and start taking a role as soon as possible.

Megan got out of her car and walked toward the building. Part of the expansion included a community room available to civic groups for meetings, presentations and programs. This would be the first time she would see the new community room and meet the members of the board of directors for the Hand in Paws Animal Clinic. Not sure why, she felt her stomach clench as she approached.

She walked up the slate steps and stepped inside to the familiar scent of old wood and books. It brought back wonderful memories of time spent there with her grandmother, picking out the books she would bring home to the cupola to read each week. Megan always looked forward to her weekly visit at the library with her grandmother.

Walking several feet into the main library room, Megan looked at the book shelves. In the corner, was a second room, enclosed with glass, decorated with colorful carpet and shelving as well as stuffed animals which represented the characters in the children's books it held. Looking toward the middle of the main room, Megan spied a counter where books, videos and e-readers were checked out. The library had been decorated with snowflakes, ornaments and bells connected to green garlands threaded around the room for the upcoming holiday season. A poster on the wall advertised a holiday literary party which was to highlight all the books with plots written around the season.

She continued walking across the main room toward the back where a modern addition had been added which housed the community room, a computer room, bathrooms and a quiet room with large expansive tables for serious students or readers who didn't want to be disturbed. There was a small counter and refrigerator which allowed patrons to fix a quick cup of tea, hot chocolate, or coffee. Next to it was a box of snacks for those who were hungry. A woman dressed in a smart business suit was fixing a cup of tea for herself. She was a handsome woman who appeared to be in her forties, with short cut brown hair and light makeup.

Megan continued down the small hallway and paused at the entrance to the community room. As her stomach rolled over, she looked through the glass panels of the door and saw several men and women inside. A few had been present at the reading of her grandmother's will, but Megan didn't know their names. Recognizing two women she did know and had always been fond of, Megan breathed a sigh of relief.

The first was Emma Smyth who had to be in her eighties. Megan remembered her to be a very sweet woman who made excellent cookies. Megan used to love to go with her grandmother to visit Emma because she would be given a plate of delicious cookies and then she would spend time with Emma's dog while the ladies talked. The dog must have passed long ago, but Megan understood why Emma would be on the board of the clinic.

The second woman she recognized was Martha Wallington. Megan didn't have as many memories of Martha and seemed to think she was involved with teaching or business. More formal and less friendly than Emma, she had been in some of the same social circles as Rose, but was always kind to Megan when they were together.

Taking a deep breath, Megan pushed the door open and entered the room. In the center of the room, was a large table around which sat many people. Teddy saw Megan's entrance and quickly stepped forward to intercept her before she sat down. He guided her to the head of the table where an empty seat waited for her presence. Teddy leaned over and said, "I'm so glad to see you here. We have much to do and it's important we get started as soon as possible."

"Okay, I'm ready when you are. Just tell me what to do," Megan whispered to Teddy.

Laughing, Teddy said, "The first thing I'd like to do is introduce you to my son. I called him, and he agreed to come to the meeting tonight, so you could get acquainted."

"Oh, great," Megan said as she followed Teddy's outstretched arm to the face of the most handsome man she'd ever met. He had sandy, blond hair and the most striking pair of blue eyes. His dress was business casual, but Megan was pretty sure his attire for tonight had been designed by Versace or Dior. She wasn't positive, but she knew the clothing had not been purchased at one of the local malls. He wore a gray suit with a white starched shirt and a cranberry tie which was held in place by a gold and diamond tie pin. Megan couldn't help but notice the gold cuff links as well. However, the clothing paled compared to the smile on his tanned face. She thought of her own clothes and her struggle to decide what to wear this evening. Most of the meetings she had gone to in the past had an attendance of four people and were held in an over-cluttered back room. The focus at the time was whose responsibility it was to bring the donuts.

Teddy waited a beat until the man walked closer and said, "Megan, I'd like you to meet my son, Jonathan Brandon Carter."

The man reached for her hand and while holding it in his softened hands, nodded a greeting. "Please, call me Jon."

Speechless for a moment, Megan almost felt dizzy as she stared into those blue eyes. "Yes, of course. My name is Megan."

"It's great to meet you, Megan. My father has told me a lot about you and your grandmother, but of course, we've met as children, haven't we?"

A voice inside Megan's head was telling her to say something, anything to respond to this man without sounding like an idiot, but her mouth remained closed as she smiled. Thankfully, Teddy came to the rescue as he broke into their brief tete-a-tete and asked them to take their seats. When they did as asked, Megan realized she was sitting at the head of the table, with Teddy to her left and Jonathan to her right. Teddy's friend, Ellen, was seated to the left of Teddy and appeared to be sorting through many documents.

Turning toward Jonathan, Megan detected a faint trace of cologne. Although she couldn't identify the brand, she knew it was expensive. Once again, she smiled as she looked into his face, without saying anything to commemorate their acquaintance.

A small bell tinkled, and Megan looked to her left to see Teddy attempting to gain the attention of those sitting around the table. "Good evening. Thank you for agreeing to meet on such short notice. I'd like to convene tonight's meeting of the board of the Hand in Paws Animal Clinic." Teddy waited for everyone to settle down and focus on the head of the table.

"As you know, we received the most disturbing news. Recently, a person or persons unknown confronted our beloved Dr. Arnie Stokes at the clinic and shot him in the back." He paused for a moment as there were murmurs and head shaking around the table. "We are unaware of motive or intent for this violation, but the police are investigating as we speak." More murmurs and whispers filled the room. "So, we have much to speak about tonight. Please take out your agendas, notepads and thinking caps so we can work together to make sure we are on the best course for our clinic."

The group spent a few minutes pulling pads, pens, folders and writing tablets out of their bags. There was a clear division between those who had all notes and documents stored digitally and those who still preferred note pads and different colored pens or highlighters to document their thoughts.

When all had settled down, Teddy took a deep breath and continued. "The first item on our agenda is to take a moment to remember our dear, departed Rose Stanford, the founder and leader of the Stanford Grants." Once again, the members of the table uttered their sympathies and shook their heads to demonstrate what a loss the grant and board had suffered.

"What a remarkable woman," Emma said. Her voice broke as she crossed herself and clasped her hands.

"Truly a loss," another man said as he frowned at the other members of the table.

"Yes, we all feel this loss on so many levels," Teddy said as he continued. "However, the fantastic news I want to share with you is that her granddaughter, Megan Stanford, is here to fulfill Rose's wishes and accept her seat as the board chair for the Hand in Paws Animal Clinic." Teddy turned toward Megan, stood up and began clapping his hands. Jonathan then stood as well as everyone else at the table and followed suit.

Megan remained in her seat, surprised, speechless and to her dismay, began crying. To see the respect and genuine love the members had for her grandmother was truly humbling and she felt very inadequate as a result. At that moment, she missed her grandmother more than she ever thought possible. She looked up when Teddy began speaking.

"Megan, we wanted to do this properly in the future. Perhaps a memorial dinner, with the proper champagne and tribute. A decision had been made to wait until you had sufficient time to grieve, although there is never a timeline on true grief, is there?" Teddy paused for a moment, swallowed and looked out at the table. "Several of the members here are on other committees involved with Stanford Grants and all want to pay proper tribute to your grandmother as a unified team. We attended Rose's funeral but have still not sufficiently memorialized her."

Megan looked around the table and recognized some of the faces from her grandmother's funeral, but everything was such a blur at that time. She realized most were probably there, grieving for her grandmother and wondering what would happen to the Stanford Grants. Megan also knew there were others from town, who were at the funeral for mere curiosity and were also wondering what would happen to Misty Manor and the rest of the Stanford estate. All would learn she had stepped into her grandmother's role. Privately, she would work hard to measure up to her grandmother, but she needed help. For that, she was glad she had Teddy and now, Jonathan at her side.

"Please, please sit down," Megan managed to say. Once everyone was seated, she continued. "Not only do I appreciate your feelings toward my grandmother, I share them with you on a daily basis. I have a lot to review regarding her committees and interests. I plan to dive into those interests as soon as I can and have greater interaction in future meetings, but for now, I simply want to thank you for your kind words and thoughts."

The group smiled, nodded and murmured good wishes. Megan turned to Teddy and said, "Please, can we move on?"

"Of course." He cleared his throat and said, "On to our next order of business. As I've said before, Dr. Stokes is currently in Coastal Community. He had some very delicate spinal surgery and has a fine neurology team caring for him now. He's in a coma, but I believe that is induced to help with healing. Until he comes out of his coma, and hopefully he will soon, we will not have any other information as to who shot him or why."

"In the meantime, we need to make arrangements for the clinic. To allow the officers to complete their investigation, we cleared out the back room of the clinic. Many of you helped to find foster parents for our furry friends until we can bring them back to the clinic or they are adopted into forever homes. Currently, the front room still houses many of our friends. We are lucky as Judy Bowan, head of the volunteers, has spent a lot of time at the clinic, organizing the other volunteers to make sure all the pets are fed, medicated and have their needs met." Teddy glanced down at a document Ellen gave to him. "Apparently, we had two dogs who recently had surgery and were moved to another animal shelter, in the next county, for more comprehensive care until we are back on our feet."

"What is our plan in the meantime?" Martha asked the group in general. "And isn't it time to start discussing next year's budget?"

"That's exactly what we need to discuss tonight," Teddy said. "Walter, I know this is an emergency meeting, but can you give us any information?" Teddy leaned over to Megan and said, "Walter Brown is our accountant. He looks over the budgets year to year as well as submitted requests and advises us of feasibility."

A man to Megan's right cleared his throat and began speaking. "Well, I have to say it's odd, because I haven't received Dr. Stoke's proposed budget yet. As you know we retained him several years ago and he's been spot on with his budgets, reports and financial requests to improve the clinic. However, he seems to have changed in the last six months. He hasn't been timely on his reports or forthcoming regarding the activity of the clinic. He hasn't submitted anything to me as of today and we obviously won't be getting anything from him now. The only thing I can do is go back to the bank and get complete statements for the last year, compare that to the supply requisitions and payments and see if we find anything." He stopped speaking and sighed. "Basically, I'm going to have to perform a complete financial audit. Nothing has seemed too out of the ordinary and he didn't have access to a large amount of money but to give you complete details, I'll have to go over everything."

Megan turned to Teddy. "Do we know anything else about Dr. Stokes? Is he married? Does he have any family?"

Teddy shook his head. "We have his initial application which does not list any family. I'm sorry to say I don't know much more about the man on a personal level. We met at his interview, several budget meetings and a few of the Stanford Christmas parties and he seemed very nice, but I've never engaged with him beyond that." Teddy shook his head and looked at Megan. "By the way, I have to talk to you about the Stanford Christmas party. It's been scheduled since last year for this weekend. We hold it at the Grand Palace. The staff and recipients of the Stanford Grants all look forward to being there. It's a lovely event. I wasn't sure if you felt up to coming but I'll give you details after tonight's meeting."

Megan nodded and whispered. "That sounds lovely. It's funny, because I was going to ask you if we had anything scheduled. There are some other things I need to go over with you as well."

"Very good," Teddy said as he turned back to hear the last of Walter's remarks. "Thank you, Walter. I know it will involve some hard work on your part, but I believe the police will be as interested in the audit as well all are."

"Yes, you'll present the information when your audit is complete?" Martha asked from her seat.

"Of course, Martha," Walter said with a tight smile.

"Well then, could you please tell me, what options we have for the clinic right now?" Emma asked with a grandmotherly smile.

"It appears there are many, Emma," Martha said testily as she looked toward the woman. "It appears we could close, either voluntarily or forced. We may have to revamp our entire approach, or we could simply hire new help and start over. Either way we have a civic responsibility to the animals we currently house and the services we provide to the town to protect against animal cruelty, abandonment and provide good veterinarian health."

Emma smiled. "Thank you, Martha dear. I believe I was asking in which direction we were leaning. I love the animals so much, I would hate to have the clinic close if we couldn't figure this out."

Martha gave a tight nod and looked away. A few other members shuffled awkwardly and looked down at the table.

Teddy broke the tension. "Actually, I've taken the liberty of reaching out to several circles I am acquainted with. It so happens they were able to suggest a replacement veterinarian who would be interested in working in the area, potentially for the clinic. I have asked her to come in this evening to be interviewed. All members of the committee who would like to meet her are invited to join us."

Megan remembered the woman at the coffee machine and realized she must be the veterinarian. Her dress and manner looked out of context with a standard library visit.

"But, before I bring her in here," Teddy said, "there are a few more items on the agenda we need to attend to."

For the next fifteen minutes the committee discussed supplies, services, potential budgets to include labor, and health benefits of staff members and their overall goals and mission. When the subject of a fundraiser was broached several people suggested different ideas involving pets and the clinic. One idea was to hold a book and bake sale in the Spring. Community members could donate books and many people were willing to bake for the event. The library would host the fundraiser in the community room and proceeds could be split between the library and the animal clinic. A woman named Agnes volunteered to take the responsibility for following up on what would be needed to run the fundraiser.

"Does anyone want to discuss anything further?" Teddy asked as he looked around the table.

Before she realized what she was doing, Megan started to speak. Her comments began haltingly, and she reddened as she discussed her idea, but she felt more comfortable as several people began to nod in agreement. "I've recently started to explore the contents of Misty Manor. With another group of people, we've discussed whether it might be nice if we restarted the Ocean Holiday Walk down the boardwalk to see the holiday lights decorating the various Victorian homes and businesses. I plan to check for some of Grandma Rose's vintage Christmas decorations. I don't think she has used any since Hurricane Sandy. Perhaps the owners of any boats in the water would be willing to decorate as well as the various docks and restaurants in the harbor. I know this committee is for the animal clinic, and I'm not sure how to segue this to the town but I thought I would bring it up here and get your thoughts."

The group was silent for a moment until they all started talking at the same moment. All seemed excited and discussed some of the former traditions.

Megan began again. "I've already talked to Tommy McDonough and he assured me that Tommy and the Tides would be willing to play music at the Christmas tree lighting if we went ahead with the idea. The Holiday Ocean Walk would end in the town square. We could advertise a Holiday by the Sea theme and have the shops remain open to sell pastries, hot chocolate and various crafts."

"I think that's a wonderful idea," Emma said excitedly as she clapped her hands. "It would be great to see more holiday spirit in the town. A Holly Berry Craft fair sounds like great fun. It's been so dark and quiet since that storm. Let's bring the spirit back and spread some love."

The others agreed with Emma and offered other suggestions to add more depth to the occasion pointing out they would have to work quickly. They all had wonderful ideas and continued to discuss the event while Martha checked with the head librarian, Heather Paris, to see if the community room was open during the week. Everyone left the meeting with great excitement and looked forward to checking their progress.

Megan stood near the end of the table with Teddy and Jonathan.

"That was phenomenal," Jonathan said as he sent a warm smile toward Megan. He turned to his father. "Are you sure she'll need me to help her navigate these meetings? It sure looked like she fired everyone up from where I sat."

Teddy was beaming as he reached out and patted her shoulder. "I am so proud of you, my dear. Not only did you survive your first committee meeting, you ignited your members in a most joyous way. Your grandmother was right. You will excel as a leader for the estate."

Megan smiled and was happy with the praise. She looked at Teddy and Jonathan and quietly said, "Most of my friends know that I've inherited Misty Manor, but I've not told anyone else about the estate. They only know I've agreed to be on Grandma Rose's committees."

"It's wise to keep it that way," Teddy said. "The public and especially local townspeople do not need to know you've inherited a two hundred-million-dollar estate. As a matter of fact, that is one of the fastest ways to lose your friends and alienate people. You'll be bothered by the financial world soon enough and there will be people in the area who'll be aware of your inheritance, but it won't be public knowledge unless you choose to make it so."

"I agree," Megan said. "I wouldn't want my friends to see me any differently than they do now. Beyond that, I don't know if I should be doing anything different, but I don't want to change who I am."

"That's a great goal," Teddy said. "But the reality is that you'll have some responsibilities and I think the next step would be for us to have a private dinner to discuss how we can ease you into the financial world." Teddy looked at Jonathan. "Let's check our calendars tomorrow and plan a dinner for yourself, Megan, Ellen and I to get to know each other better."

"Of course," Jonathan said. "I have a couple of business meetings, but I'll make sure Ellen has some solid dates to work with." He then turned to Megan and flashed a tummy warmer smile. "Of course, it's all dependent on your availability."

"Of course," Megan said as she heard her own voice squeak.

CHAPTER 20

"Am I late?" Megan quickly looked up at the voice and realized Nick had walked into the community room. Not quite understanding why, her face reddened when she saw him there.

"Hey Nick," Megan said, with a tremor in her voice. "Late for what?"

"The meeting," Nick said as he walked over to the group. Megan noticed he looked very handsome in his pressed jeans and well fitted polo shirt.

"The board meeting just ended," Megan said as she turned to Teddy for support.

Teddy paused for a moment before he spoke, "I invited Nick to be with us tonight for the interview. I had a conversation with the police this afternoon. While I was answering their questions, I explained we were planning on interviewing a possible veterinarian to take over for Dr. Stokes. If we don't hire someone quickly, I fear we'll have to close the clinic which would not be in anyone's best interest."

"Okay, but I'm still not following," Megan said as she watched Nick stand beside Jonathan. The two nodded at each other when Jonathan extended his hand as a way of introduction. Megan felt her stomach clench as her two worlds collided but really wasn't sure why.

Teddy continued to explain. "Part of the process was understanding Dr. Stokes's role in the clinic and Nick thought it may be helpful to be part of the interview with the new veterinarian to get a better grasp of the position."

"Fine, that's great," Megan said as she looked around the room. No one else from the committee had stayed for the interview. When they were ready, Ellen led the woman in the business suit into the room and seated her in a chair on one end of the table across from Teddy, Jonathan, Nick, Ellen and herself.

Teddy began speaking while Ellen passed over copies of her resume. "Good evening and thank you for coming to meet us so quickly."

"My pleasure and I'm excited to be interviewing for this position," she said as she confidently smiled at the group before her.

Teddy introduced everyone in the room and then said, "Why don't you start with telling us about yourself?"

The woman took a deep breath and clasped her hands on top of the table. She looked up, smiled and said, "Hi, my name is Dr. April May and I'm from New York. I've been a veterinarian for five years now."

Teddy looked up and said, "I see you got your degree from Cornell?"

"Yes, I did," she said as she nodded.

"That's wonderful," Teddy said. "What have you been doing for the last five years?"

"I was employed as a veterinarian in a large practice serving the Midwest. We cared for large animals including equine and farm animals. Most of our work was done on the road with an ambulatory service based on the needs of different farms and stables."

"That's very interesting," Megan said. "I've never thought about veterinarians making house calls."

April smiled. "I assure you we do. We work very hard to keep these animals healthy due to their high value."

"It sounds like it could be stressful," Nick said as he listened to her speak.

"Yes, it can be very stressful. There is no room for failure, but sadly not every illness can be cured. Not every infection can be treated."

"Is that why you left? Or I guess I should ask, have you left?" Megan asked, eyebrows raised.

"Yes, I have officially left that job and returned to the East Coast, but the reason I left was because I was becoming tired of working in a different location each week. I wanted steady work and job security. As a vet, you become attached to certain farms or animals and it would be nice to be in a steady place, month after month. Also, it's nice to be able to follow up with your treatments. To find out if they worked and check on the status of the animals. Jumping around can be tedious."

Teddy asked the next question. "New Jersey seems a long way from the Midwest and I'm not sure how many farm animals we have in New Jersey."

April laughed. She had a nice full laugh as if amused by life. "Actually, you'd be surprised at how many farm animals live in New Jersey. However, the number of veterinarians in New Jersey who are officially trained for farms is fewer than you would think."

"You are aware the Hand in Paws Animal Clinic does not see any farm animals that I know of," Teddy said. "Not to say we couldn't if we needed to, but traditionally we see small animals such as dogs, cats, and rabbits. Would working in a clinic like that interest you?"

"Yes, I believe it would," April said immediately. "For one thing, it would be a nice change of pace. I've always loved small animals and I've never seen a farm without them. Secondly, and this is something I was going to bring up later, I would like to offer my services to some of the local horse farms. There are many in New Jersey and I enjoy working with horses."

"Very interesting," Teddy said as he nodded. "Are you living in New Jersey or are you back in New York?"

"I'm living in New Jersey," April May said. "My father lives here. I was born and raised in New York, near New Paltz. After my mom died, my father moved to New Jersey to be closer to his sister. She's a widow and they help take care of each other, but need extra support. I was looking for a change of pace and thought I could help them and find different work as well."

"Your dad is Mr. May?" Megan had been dying to ask the question since she heard April announce herself but couldn't quite find a way to verbalize it without sounding too personal. She knew she had no right to ask about age, but April May appeared to be the same age as Megan. There was no wedding ring on her finger.

"Yes, Ralph May," April said as she laughed. "And before you burst from curiosity, the answer is yes, my real full name is April May. That's what's listed on my birth certificate and social security card. I am told my mother loved a song which listed the months and asked to name me April despite marrying a man whose last name was May."

"Were you teased in school?" Megan asked to lighten the atmosphere.

"The kids were very accepting of my name, but heads do turn each time I introduce myself."

"Thank you," Megan said. "I didn't mean to take away from your interview."

"Perfectly fine," she said as she waved her hand to the side.

"What questions do you have for us?" Teddy asked as he looked at April.

"Please tell me more about this position. What does it entail? Why is it available and why in such a hurry?"

"I'd be happy to," Teddy said as he cleared his throat. Those sitting around him shifted and looked at each other, unsure how much should be said.

"The Hand in Paws Animal Clinic was opened several years ago through a grant underwritten by Mrs. Rose Stanford. She has passed now, but Megan is her granddaughter and will be carrying on in her place. Until now, the clinic has served as a shelter as well as clinic for animals that are abandoned, or need routine care, immunizations and boarding. It is strictly a no kill shelter and we will search to help find every animal a home. We've had adoptions from out of state, wherever a loving home can be found, and we research every adoption before it's approved."

Teddy paused and took a breath. "Dr. Arnie Stokes has been our veterinarian since the clinic opened, however he was recently a victim of a shooting. This area does not have a lot of crime, however some of the surrounding neighborhoods are not places you'd want to be alone in at night. To be honest, we don't know why or how this happened and to be fair, we don't know if it was random or targeted."

"Do you have security in the clinic?" April asked looking at Teddy with wide eyes.

"We do," Teddy assured her. "Our doors have digital locks. Every entrance is alarmed and there are cameras in each room." Teddy paused for a moment. "Not that we've needed to use them, and we've never had a police involved situation in the past, but the security is certainly up to code. However, I wanted to be fair and let you know exactly what's going on. You'll hear rumors and gossip from volunteers and owners. It appears Dr. Stokes will not be coming back to the clinic for a while and we have quite a few animals housed there. We have a responsibility to those animals and need someone to care for them, as soon as possible, which is why your interview has been expedited."

"Can I break in here?" The group turned their heads to look at Nick as he spoke to April. "To be honest, I'm a town police officer and someone who supports the clinic."

Megan frowned for just a second. She hadn't realized Nick had been connected to the clinic before a few days ago. She turned back and focused on his words. He was posing a question to the veterinarian.

"I was wondering if I could ask you about what happened in the clinic? Are you aware of any reason why an animal clinic would be targeted?"

April nodded her head several times. "Actually, there are many reasons why clinics need to be careful today. The first is drugs." April spread her hands as she spoke and was prepared to conquer the topic. "Being in New Jersey, I don't need to spend any time talking about the opioid crisis. Now that doctors are limited in the pain killers they prescribe, people are turning to animal clinics. We often have pets in discomfort and veterinarians use many of the same pain meds and narcotics as doctors do with humans. There have been reports of animal owners bringing their pets in for pain or purposely harming their pets to obtain opioids."

"I have to admit, I had not known that," Megan said, surprised at April's explanation.

"Yes, and there are other reasons," April continued. "We use many of the same supplies for surgeries. Often supplies are targeted for use in gangs whose members cannot be seen in a hospital for injuries."

"Very interesting," Nick said. "Anything else?"

"Yes, and these reasons are a bit more gruesome. Pets go missing all the time and for several reasons. Well-groomed pets from certain breeds are targeted, stolen and then resold on the black market to different owners. There is a black market for animals. Unfortunately, some are sold to medical schools or pharmaceutical companies for experimentation. Some animals are simply stolen because the would-be owner can't afford the adoption fees.

"I can understand the adoption fees," Nick said. "I've heard certain breeds are sold for thousands of dollars."

"That's absolutely true," April said as she offered a warm smile to Nick.

Jonathan cleared his throat to bring attention back to the interview at hand. "Your statements are very sobering, but we don't know if any of those reasons were involved in this particular shooting. Perhaps we can return to our task tonight. Do you have any other questions for us?"

"Yes, I was wondering about hours and whether I could see the clinic. Of course, we would have to discuss compensation and benefits as well."

"Of course, completely understandable," Jonathan said.

"I have an idea," Teddy said as he pulled out a pocket watch and checked the time. "It's getting rather late. Why don't we adjourn for the night and meet tomorrow at the clinic? We can offer a tour and I'd be able to discuss your salary and benefits in detail, after I speak with Ms. Stanford, of course."

April looked at Megan for a moment and agreed.

"Wonderful," Teddy said as he looked up at Dr. May. "I believe you have the address and may I suggest we meet at 10:00 a.m.?" He then turned to Megan. "Is that a good time for you?"

Megan didn't respond at first and then realized Teddy was waiting for her to agree. "Oh, yes, that's fine."

"Excellent, well then, let's be off, and we'll see everyone in the morning."

"Thank you for coming in," Megan said as she stood and walked over to shake April's hand. "I learned quite a bit from your interview."

"It's a pleasure to meet you and I hope we get the chance to work together," April said as she smiled at Megan.

"I'm sure things will work out. I'll see you tomorrow." Megan turned and was surprised to find Nick waiting for her as well as Jonathan standing behind him. Teddy and Ellen stood off to the side. Not knowing what to do, she turned back to April and said, "Can we walk you out?"

The group walked out of the library together and into the parking lot. Once there, they began to drift toward their separate cars. They paused and watched as Dr. May climbed into a SUV and drove off. Megan was glad it wasn't her as she knew it was awkward to have everyone watching. She turned as Teddy called her name. "Perhaps we can meet at 9:00 a.m. to discuss a few things before our next meeting with Dr. May?"

"Of course," Megan said.

"I'll drop by the house in the morning and we can talk before we go to the clinic."

"Wonderful, I'll have the coffee ready," Megan said.

"It was delightful meeting you tonight," Jonathan said as he smiled. "I'm afraid I can't be at the meeting tomorrow morning, but I'd like to get together as soon as possible."

"I look forward to it," Megan said as Jonathan took her hand once again and gave it a squeeze. When he let her hand go, Jonathan turned to Teddy and Ellen and together they walked toward their cars.

Megan turned back and found Nick at her side. She looked up at him when he said, "What's up?"

She laughed and shook her head. "Nothing much, just learning how to be the chairwoman of the board of a local animal clinic."

Nick nodded toward the now empty parking lot as they walked toward her car. "Who was the fancy suit?'

"Who?" Megan asked, teasing him. "I didn't notice anyone. It's a beautiful night, isn't it?"

"Yeah, right," Nick said. "Who was that?"

Megan laughed as she turned toward him. "Believe it or not, that was Teddy's son, Jonathan Brandon Carter."

"What? I never knew Teddy had a son."

"It's funny you say that because I wouldn't have remembered Teddy's son either, but Teddy reminded me we had played together as children."

"What?" Nick said, now even more incredulous.

"It's true," Megan said. "I remembered the day, and the boy, but I didn't realize it was Teddy's son until he pointed it out to me." They had arrived at Megan's car.

"I don't remember any strangers living in Misty Point when we were young," Nick said as he leaned in closer to Megan's face.

"Well, there's a little bit of a story," Megan said as she felt her back up against the door. Her breath caught as Nick leaned closer. "I could tell you all about it."

"Why don't we save it for another time," Nick said as his arms went around her waist.

Megan felt his warm breath against her cheek and within seconds his lips had found hers. Their first kiss was warm and soft, but the second was longer and deeper and took Megan's breath away.

When Nick pulled away he smiled and said, "I've missed you."

Megan grinned. "I've missed you, too."

"Why don't we go for a little ride before you go home? It's a beautiful night and warm for December. Maybe we can stop at the boardwalk and listen to the water for a while."

Megan felt her belly warming at his suggestion, but shook her head. "I actually have two animals waiting for me at the house. I need to go home and let Dudley out."

Nick groaned and put his head on her shoulder. "Really?"

"Yes, really, it's been hours," Megan said as she nuzzled his neck. "Unless you want to visit me at the house?"

Nick pulled back and frowned. "I have to be at work very early in the morning. As much as I'd like to spend the night, I'd better go home."

Megan sighed. "If you insist."

"Don't make this harder than it is, Megan." Nick said as he held her around the waist.

"I won't, Nick, but I'd really better go," Megan said as she moved to the side and opened her car door.

"I'll call you tomorrow," Nick said as he gave her a peck on the cheek.

"I look forward to hearing from you," Megan whispered with a smile as she slid into the car and fastened her seat belt. When she was done, Nick closed the car door and tapped on the window. He stepped back when Megan started the car, backed out of her space and drove away.

CHAPTER 21

Megan walked up the porch steps and to the front door. She paused for a moment and looked behind her. The wind was still, and the weather was warm for a December night. The crash of the surf was loud. Megan looked up. The full moon was approaching so the water seemed higher than normal. Perhaps she should have accepted the car ride with Nick. It would have been nice to cuddle near the beach and be able to clear her mind of the events of the last two days.

Turning back to the door, Megan readied her key when she heard whimpering. Not sure what the noise was about, she paused and listened. After a moment, she realized Dudley was at the door. He must have heard her coming.

Megan called his name and she heard him bark in response. She opened the door as quickly as she could, reached inside and flicked on the foyer lights. Dudley was before her, excitedly turning circles and nudging her hand for attention. Megan dropped to a knee and rubbed his head.

"Are you okay?" Megan received a bevy of dog kisses in return. Laughing she sat back on her bottom and looked at the dog. He seemed okay and was very happy she was home. "Is Smokey okay?"

She stood up and walked into the kitchen. Smokey was curled up in the dog bed, in the corner between the refrigerator and the cabinets. Megan knew that part of the kitchen had the benefit of warm air which blew out from under the refrigerator.

"You two were so good while I was gone," Megan said to the animals. As she went to the pantry to get them each a treat, her cell phone vibrated in her back pocket. She pulled it out and recognized Georgie's cell.

"Hey, how are you?" She asked as she answered the call.

"We're fine," Georgie said. "We're in your driveway with a pizza and some beer. Open up the front door."

"You've got it," Megan said as she walked to the door.

Dudley followed her as soon as he sucked down his doggie cookie. She told him to behave as she opened the door and Georgie and Amber stepped inside. Dudley immediately began wagging his tail and Megan assumed he smelled the pizza.

"C'mon back. We're in the kitchen," she said as she guided her friends down the foyer hall. They all sat at the table. Georgie passed a beer for each of them and opened the box.

"Isn't this the second time we've had pizza today?" Megan asked.

"I know, but I love it," Georgie said. "In all fairness, we asked for extra meatball on this one so it would add more protein. Honestly, I could eat pizza every day, especially if I rotated the toppings or salad I ate with it."

"In that case, I hope you never stop running," Megan said.

"I'm glad you said it," Amber said as she choose one slice and then ripped it in half.

"Good, more for me," Georgie said as she looked at her friend. "Have you even had five hundred calories today?"

"Oh, shut up," Amber said as she bit into her small slice like it was the yummiest treat she had ever had. "You don't have to worry about corporate clothes."

"Oh, speaking of clothes," Megan said as wiped her mouth with the back of her hand. "I might have to ask you to help me go shopping."

Amber and Georgie both stopped eating and looked at her. "Who are you and what have you done with our friend?" Amber said as she grabbed her fork. "Tell us right now and we won't hurt you."

"Oh, stop it. I simply asked you to help me shop for some clothes and you two go nuts."

"You never want to shop, and I don't think you've worn more than jeans since you've come home," Amber said.

"Busted," Georgie said while pulling a string of cheese from her mouth. "Does it have something to do with your meeting tonight? By the way, that's the reason we dropped by. We want to know what happened."

Megan picked up another slice of pizza. She thoughtfully chewed and swallowed before she answered. "It was very interesting." She picked up her beer and took a small sip. Megan took a few minutes to tell them about the meeting and interview with Dr. April May, the veterinarian. "At some point, I'm going to nominate both of you to be on some of these committees with me."

"Yea, well save me for a committee that has to do with keeping the beach clean and protecting the ocean," Georgie said as she closed the pizza box lid.

"Forget the committees," Amber said. "I want to hear more about Jonathan."

"He was something," Megan said with a tilt to her head. "Very cultured, nice suit, white starched shirt, with cuff links, no buttons."

"Cuff links?" Amber asked with wide eyes.

"Yes, cuff links," Megan said again.

"I can't wait to meet this guy," Amber said. "He sounds dreamy."

Georgie started laughing. "I get it and what did you wear? Jeans and a fancy t-shirt?"

"Don't be a jerk. I don't know what to wear to a meeting. I didn't expect everyone to be dressed up."

"Well you're right," Amber said. "We need to go clothes shopping. You'll also need shoes, a purse and a few other things. Do you even have a nice coat?"

"Oh," Megan groaned. "I hate shopping and dressing up."

"Listen, I'm sure your grandmother always represented herself properly. If you want to fill the image, you must wear the proper clothes, shoes and everything else. Wow, I may have to give you lessons on behavior as well."

"I'm supposed to be receiving lessons from Jonathan on running an estate."

"Well, that may be the one course I'd be happy to go back to school for," Amber said with a wicked grin.

"You better not let Tommy hear you say that," Georgie said.

"C'mon, I'm dating, not dead," Amber said. "I've never had to work so hard at a relationship."

"And what about Nick?" Georgie asked as she turned to Megan.

"What about Nick?" Megan said. "Listen, I just think I should have more professional clothes. That's all I said, and I thought you two would want to go to the mall with me."

"I'm in," Amber said. "Anytime, anywhere, girlfriend. Just make sure it's after my work hours."

"I'll go too," Georgie said.

"Great to hear that," Amber said. "There's a fancy trend out now for women. I'd like to show it to you. It's called a dress."

Georgie wadded up a napkin and threw it at Amber. "Shut up."

"And while we're out, we need to get a few things for the holidays. Maybe a little red dress?" Amber suggested.

"That's a clever idea, because Teddy told me the Stanford Christmas party is this weekend and you'll be invited. Let's bring Tommy, Nick and whoever else we think of."

Amber jumped up and down and clapped her hands. "This is so exciting and then we have to start putting up the Christmas decorations, so we can get ready for the Ocean Holiday Walk and Christmas tree lighting."

Georgie scowled at her friend.

Megan shook her head, stood up and cleaned the table.

CHAPTER 22

*E*arly the next morning, Nick showed up at the police station with a bag full of donuts and two large paper cups of coffee. He walked around the front desk and toward the Chief's office.

Looking through the glass pane, Nick pushed the door open with his foot and stepped inside. Davis sat behind his desk. He was talking on the phone, an unhappy expression on his face. Nick set the donut bag and cups on the desk and pushed one of the coffees toward his boss. He opened the bag and pulled out four donuts. Two Boston cream and two chocolate frosted with sprinkles. He placed one of each kind on a napkin and pushed it toward his boss as well.

While listening to someone speak, Davis gave a thumbs up, and pulled the coffee and donuts toward his side of the desk. Without hesitation, he held the phone against his shoulder, cracked open the plastic lid on the steaming coffee and took a bite of the Boston cream. After a few seconds, he said, "Well, get on it as fast as you can and call me back with the results. I have everyone breathing down my neck." He then took the phone off his shoulder and hung up before he helped himself to another bite. "Bastards, they're stonewalling me already."

"Forensics?" Nick asked as he took a gulp of coffee.

"It's the crime scene investigator," Davis said. "I'm trying to get an idea of what kind of trace we found so I can follow up. Everything is a song and dance." He picked up the chocolate donut and finished it off in four bites. Crumbs around his mouth, he nodded and said, "Thanks Nick, I needed that."

"No problem," Nick said. "If it puts you in a good mood, it's worth it."

"The only thing that's gonna help my mood is getting some traction on this case," Davis said as he gulped his coffee, but not without spilling a few drops on his white shirt. "Damn," he said as he wiped at the brown liquid which caused it to absorb into the fabric. "Aww, screw it."

Davis looked up at Nick. "So where do we stand? Did you get any info last night?"

Nick shook his head as he pondered his coffee. "I took a shift at the hospital, but there's nothing going on over there. At 9:00 p.m., one of the volunteers from the clinic showed up to see how Dr. Stokes was, but they turned him away."

"Kind of late for a concerned friend to be visiting someone in the hospital, isn't it?" Davis watched Nick over the desk.

"You'd be surprised how much activity goes on in a hospital at night. The place didn't quiet down until 11:30 p.m. The guy is on camera though. We're recording everyone who asks a question or even has an interest in the case."

"So, what happened?"

"He left some flowers and walked away," Nick said. "Dr. Stokes is still sedated and will stay that way until he shows a certain level of healing."

"Get an identification. We must look at all the volunteers and even the regulars dropping off donations. Whoever was there knew the routine, knew the clinic and most likely knew the cameras weren't working." Davis shook his head and tossed a napkin into the garbage pail. "We have to figure out what's going on with this clinic and catch this bastard."

"Let's go over what we already know," Nick said while biting a donut.

"We know several clinics have been hit throughout the county in the last couple months," Davis said. "The State Police are comparing data from each place. They want to see if any of them have the same volunteers, donors, or patients visiting multiple places. They haven't had time to add the names of the people from Hand in Paws into the database yet. A few places have video, but we've got nothing to compare it to, but someone will run through it anyway."

"Any patterns so far?"

"No patterns of what was stolen, or who was hit or when except they were all animal clinics. On the other hand, the county has an uptick of gas stations getting hit as well. So who knows, what's related to what?"

"We're placing someone undercover," Nick said. "Maybe the perps will return to the scene of the crime."

"Not likely, they'll know we're watching if we don't pull out soon," Davis said as he scowled. "You didn't tell your girlfriend you were on watch at the hospital, did you?"

"I haven't told Megan anything," Nick said as he bristled. "She was surprised I was at the interview last night, but she didn't press me."

"It's better that way," Davis said. "She can't let slip what she doesn't know. It's safer for her."

Nick frowned. "Maybe. I'm going over to the clinic this morning. They're having a tour to see if they can sign a new veterinarian. If so, they'll have new staff in place and can resume activities."

"Well get over there and let me know what the hell is going on," Davis said as his desk phone started ringing. "Davis," he yelled as he picked up the receiver and held it to his ear. Nick waited to see if the call was significant, but Davis shook his head and waved for Nick to move on.

CHAPTER 23

*M*egan woke up in the morning on her right side. She leaned backward to roll over and felt a warm body against her back. Within seconds of moving, she felt warm breath near her face as well as a warm tongue on her cheek.

"Ugh," Megan said as she wiped Dudley's saliva off her cheek. She tried but initially couldn't move her legs as Smokey was settled in between her calves. "What the hell? Sorry guys or gals or whatever, but it's my bed and I'd like to be able to stretch out. I thought I left you in the kitchen. I don't know how you come in this room at night without waking me, but this is nuts."

Megan rolled to her left and Dudley got up and jumped off the bed. Smokey rearranged himself in a different position near the edge of the bed. Megan rolled onto her back and waited a few seconds to let her muscles relax. After a minute or so, she pulled off the covers and got out of bed. As soon as her feet hit the floor, Dudley jumped up, helped Smokey off the bed and stood near the door, wagging his tail in anticipation of being let outside to do his business and returning to a delicious breakfast. Megan looked at the dog. "Sorry, but before I go down three flights of stairs, I have to make a stop of my own."

The animals waited by the bathroom, each of them peeking around the door. "Hey, how about a little privacy?"

Dudley wagged his tail until Megan walked out of the bathroom while Smokey was more curious and did a little investigation of his own.

"Let's go." Megan headed toward the grand staircase and the pets followed her. She reached the foyer at the bottom and turned towards the kitchen as they flew by in anticipation of their breakfast.

Thirty minutes later, the animals had been fed and Dudley went outside to do his business. Megan made a pot of strong, rich coffee and was pouring her second cup when the doorbell rang. Dudley raced out to the foyer and was standing guard when Megan opened the front door to let Teddy inside.

"Good morning," Megan said as she took his coat. "I just made a pot of coffee. Would you like a cup?"

"Sounds excellent," Teddy said. "It's colder today and the wind is blowing inland."

Megan noticed Teddy was dressed more casually today. "Would you mind sitting in the kitchen?"

"Of course not," Teddy said. "I spent a good amount of time talking about things with your grandmother in the kitchen, especially when she was baking."

Megan smiled. She didn't have a lot of memories of her grandmother in the kitchen, but did remember her making Christmas cookies. Grandma Rose made a delicious dough and together they had cut out cookies in the shapes of sea shells and stars. Megan made a mental note to look for her grandmother's recipe box and add baking cookies to the list of holiday preparation.

"I'm glad we're having this meeting before we go to the clinic," Teddy said. "I didn't want to make any commitments last night until we had time to have an official business meeting."

"There's so much I have to learn," Megan said as she placed a coffee mug in front of Teddy and poured a steaming cup of coffee. She placed cream, sugar, a spoon and napkin before him as she had no idea of how he liked his coffee, but she was sure her grandmother knew. "Until I have time to get up to speed, I'll defer all vital decisions to you. I'll need time to study my grandmother's methods, but I have a decent business sense of my own."

"Thank you, I appreciate it," Teddy said as he tasted the delicious coffee.

"Have you eaten?" Megan asked as she placed a plate of muffins in front of him.

"Yes, I did, thank you. I'm on a strict diet, no fat, minimal carbohydrates and those are always natural not processed."

Megan placed the coffee pot on the table and sat down. She felt guilty as she thought back to the donut she popped in her mouth while she waited for the animals to finish their breakfast.

"Anyway, once we have the tour, you can let me know if you're satisfied with this veterinarian. I've located a local assistant for her and I asked him to be there this morning as well. His name is Carlos Sanchez. I reviewed his resume and I think it will be safer for our new doctor to have an assistant by her side."

"That's a great idea," Megan said. "Plus, I would assume she'd need help with the exams and lifting the animals on and off the table."

"Absolutely, although our modern tables do move up and down for convenience."

Megan nodded. "That makes sense. I've never really watched anyone work in an animal clinic before, so this is all new to me."

Teddy pursed his lips and nodded in silence. After a moment, he spoke. "Megan, your grandmother didn't understand every aspect of every charity, but she was a great judge of character. She had a strong intuition as to whether someone was a good fit for a Stanford Grant." Teddy looked at her and smiled. "I'm sincerely hoping that is one of the qualities you inherited from her, because it was a vital piece of her work."

Megan refilled Teddy's cup and chuckled. "I guess time will tell, no pressure though."

"I didn't mean to pressure you. I'm trying to share how we worked together in the past."

"And I appreciate that. I really do, Teddy. This whole business has shocked me back to my senses somewhat. Between coming home and Rose dying, I've been drifting through day to day. We need to get through this business with the animal clinic, get through the holidays and then I'll concentrate on an action plan for all the charities as well as Misty Manor. I promise."

"I'm so glad to hear that. Jonathan will help guide you. He's a nice guy and won't steer you wrong."

"I'm sure of that," Megan said, her hands wrapped around her warm cup. "I'm more worried about my role and understanding what I need to know."

Teddy reached out and patted Megan's hand. "Just having your grandmother's personality will be enough to win the day. I promise you that."

"Thank you, Teddy. Let's hope I eventually live up to her standards. So, what did you specifically want to cover today?" Megan sipped her coffee and made sure the animals were content in the corner of the kitchen.

"I wanted to make sure you're comfortable with me discussing salaries and the benefit arrangements. There are legal aspects to hiring and they're a bit different in a grant situation."

"I am absolutely fine with that," Megan said. "I wouldn't have a clue where to start."

Teddy drained his cup. "The coffee was excellent." He looked at his watch. "We still have a little time. Do you want me to drive you to the clinic?"

"No, I want to run upstairs and change. Also, I thought I'd bring Dudley with me. Eventually, the two animals will go back when this mess is settled so he should visit on occasion. Smokey can stay here while we go."

Teddy smiled as he got out of his chair and headed toward the front door. "Okay, I'll see you at the clinic at 10:00 a.m. Thanks again for the coffee."

Megan handed him his coat. "You're most welcome." She and the dog watched as he left the porch and headed toward his car.

CHAPTER 24

$\mathcal{M}$egan pulled up to the curb in front of the clinic and parked the car. Once Teddy left, she ran upstairs and quickly showered and changed. She asked Dudley if he would like to ride with her and before she could blink he had his leash in his mouth and was standing out by the car. She opened the door and he jumped in the backseat and sat down. He happily panted watched the scenery go by during the short ride to the clinic.

Turning off the ignition, she unclipped her seatbelt and slid out of the car. She then opened the door behind her and Dudley hopped out, wagging his tail and still holding his leash in his mouth. They walked across the lawn and entered the clinic by the back door. Inside, she found Dr. April May, Teddy, Nick and another gentleman she didn't recognize.

"Nick, what are you doing here?" Megan asked as she approached the small group. Nick was standing next to April and chatting quite amicably.

"Teddy said the tour was at 10:00 a.m. so I came by. I figure the more I know about normal routine, the better chance I have of trying to figure out who's doing this and why."

"Oh, that makes sense," Megan said. She held on to Dudley's leash as he stood amongst the group.

"Megan, I'm so glad you're here," Teddy said as he welcomed her to the group. "I believe you know everyone except Mr. Sanchez." Teddy took a moment to introduce Carlos to everyone in the group. He was a muscular man, fluent in Spanish and English.

"Very nice to meet you," Megan said. "Do you have a lot of experience working in an animal clinic?"

"Yes, Ma'am," Carlos said. "I've worked as a veterinary assistant since college. I'm very excited about this opportunity." Carlos bent down to pet Dudley whose tail was wagging.

"I'm sure you'll be a powerful addition to the clinic," Megan said as she looked at Teddy. "Why don't we get started."

Teddy spent the next forty-five minutes touring them through the small building. They started the tour in the front room where several volunteers were feeding and cleaning out cages. One of the volunteers recognized Dudley and approached him. She dropped to one knee and rubbed his head. He responded by licking her face and wagging his tail.

"Would you like me to watch him for you? You look like you're busy."

Megan watched Dudley with the girl. "That would be great, if you're free. I have a few things I have to do."

"No problem. Just come back whenever you're ready to leave. I'm sure he'll enjoy visiting his friends."

"Oh, will do," Megan said as she handed the leash to the girl who led Dudley away.

Within seconds, Teddy drew her attention back to the group and continued the tour. He explained the history, mission and function of the building as they walked.

"Hand in Paws Animal Clinic serves as a shelter for animals who are abandoned or lost, and as a clinic for animals to receive immunizations and basic care, such as spaying and neutering. That would be your department, Dr. May. We also help animals find their forever homes and serve as a small emergency clinic for animals with problems."

Dr. April May looked around. "What type of emergency equipment or supplies do you have here? And please call me April."

"Yes, of course, April," Teddy answered. "We have a small trauma area, complete with an x-ray machine, ultrasound equipment and capability for minor surgery, intravenous solutions, and medications."

"May I see that area?"

"Yes, please follow me." Teddy led them to a rear room which held a small operating table as well as all the supplies to perform surgery and suture in a sterile setting. Next, he showed them the supply room where all expensive medication and narcotics were kept. He opened the safe to demonstrate how it worked as he discussed the procedure to log all medications that were received, ordered and dispensed.

Teddy stopped talking when he realized the safe was empty. He turned to Nick. "Did you take anything from here?"

"Me?" Nick asked. Surprise shadowed his expression.

"No, not you specifically, but did the police take the rest of the inventory as part of the investigation? The safe is empty, but it was full of narcotics and other pain medications yesterday."

"If it was there when our investigation started, it should be there now. We don't remove property of the clinic unless there is a specific reason for it and even then, we would have logged it into evidence. I'll check the log just to be sure, but I highly doubt it."

"Then we have a problem," Teddy said.

"Are the cameras working?" Nick asked, looking around.

"We haven't been able to get a representative from the security company in here, yet," Teddy answered as he shook his head.

"How about the safe? Has the combination been changed?"

"We haven't done anything," Teddy said. "I wasn't sure we were cleared to change things."

Nick popped into full police mode. "Okay, then let's report it as another theft." He pulled out his cell. "I'll make the report. Don't touch anything else. Let's let the team dust the area and see if any new prints showed up." As he waited for someone to pick up the phone, he continued to speak to Teddy. "I'll need you to make a list of what was in that safe. Do you have a log or inventory sheet?"

"Yes, there is a log sheet, somewhere. The rules in a veterinary clinic are not as strict as the regular healthcare field so I don't know how accurate it is. I can look at the purchase orders, but I'm not sure if Dr. Stokes documented what he recently used so, once again, I'm not sure how accurate it would be."

"Who would have had access to this room in the last forty-eight hours?"

Teddy paused for a moment as the group watched. "I guess anyone who's been in the building. The door to the supply room was left unlocked, so any volunteer or person working or visiting the building could have wandered in here, but the last group I saw working in here was the CSI team. I'm not sure when they left or how they left it, so I'm also not sure how long there's been unrestricted access. At any rate, only those that have the combination to the safe would be able to get in there."

"Look around the supply area. Is there anything missing in this room?"

"I don't know," Teddy said, shaking his head.

"Wouldn't the CSI team have taken photos of the whole room?" Megan asked. "Why don't they come back, take more photos and then compare them? Until then and after, let's keep the door locked and change the combination to the safe."

"Yes, I agree that sounds like a great idea," Teddy said. "Apparently, there is no stock for the safe now anyway and I don't believe there are any orders on the way. Everything was put on hold until we straighten this whole mess out."

Teddy turned to April. "I'm horrified to have your tour of the clinic be this way. We've never had a problem like this that I'm aware of. I hope you'll still consider taking the job. It's obvious we need someone to take charge here."

"I understand," April said. "When you have a moment, we need to talk about salary, hours and benefits. I feel better knowing Carlos would be working with me as well."

"Thank you so much. Perhaps we can go into one of the offices and talk this over. Is that okay with you Nick?"

"Absolutely," Nick said. "The less traffic in here, the better."

Teddy turned to April and Carlos. "Shall we then?"

After the group left, Megan turned to Nick. "What's going on? I'm starting to think there's much more of an issue here, especially because you've been a part of everything. What aren't you telling me?"

Nick looked at Megan, but didn't say anything.

"Talk to me, Nick. My name is all over this and I have no clue what's going on. Tell me."

"Okay, but I'm not supposed to be talking about an investigation." Nick said with a frown.

"We've shared information before and as I recall it was helpful to solve the case." Megan placed her hand on her hip.

"Okay, but don't tell anyone I told you anything and don't repeat it. Davis is up in arms about the shooting because there's been a rash of robberies at animal clinics in the area lately. They all seem to involve narcotics or missing dogs, but we really don't have a good handle on what's going on. It seems larger than a one-person attack. No one else has been harmed so we assume Dr. Stokes saw something he shouldn't have which resulted in him getting shot."

"Then he would still be in danger when he wakes up," Megan said.

"Yes, because he may be able to identify a person of interest for us, if he remembers what happened at all." Megan went to speak but Nick cut her off. "Yes, before you ask, we do have officers watching his room in case someone tries anything."

"Okay, just checking," Megan said as she crossed her arms. "So, then the Hand in Paws clinic was not specifically targeted?"

"Possibly not," Nick whispered in the supply room.

"That makes me feel better," Megan said. "Maybe I should tell Teddy."

Nick scowled. "What did I just say? You promised not to tell anyone else. Do you want me fired?"

Megan reached out and touched Nick's arm. "No, of course not. Okay, mums the word, but if you get to a point where we can let Teddy know, I think he would appreciate the information."

"You got it," Nick said as he placed his hands around Megan's waist. He pulled her close and kissed her lightly.

"Excuse me," Megan teased. "Did you actually just kiss me in the supply closet?"

"You know I did," Nick grinned. "I'd try again if I thought it was safe."

Right on cue, Judy Bowan, the volunteer supervisor opened the door to the supply closet. She was wearing her green smock with the doggie paws on it. "Oh, I'm sorry," she said as she looked at Nick and Megan in an embrace. "I don't think I've had to worry about anyone in a closet in years." She chuckled to herself. "I hope you don't mind but I need some of these bandages for one of our dogs out there. She had surgery the day Dr. Stokes was, well, you know. Anyway, someone still has to change her bandages."

Nick and Megan pulled apart. "Excuse us," Megan said.

"Oh, it's okay, Dearie. I've had my share of trysts in a closet," Judy said as she laughed to herself.

Nick cleared his throat. "Judy, I'd like to ask you a question."

"Ok, shoot," she said as she waited with a package of gauze in her hand.

"Do the volunteers come in here often?"

"Only if they must," Judy said with a tight smile. "We used to help Dr. Stokes get supplies and prepare for scheduled surgeries."

"Do any of the volunteers go into the safe?"

"That's not for us," Judy said as she shook her head. "We're not allowed to touch the medicines unless we give vitamins to the animals or something like that. But even then, Dr. Stokes would hand it to us. We didn't take them."

"Okay, thanks," Nick said as the door swung open again. Officer Peters was at the door. "Hey, what is this a party?"

"I'm leaving right now," Megan said.

"Me too," Judy sang out as she walked out of the room in front on Megan.

Megan looked back in the room. "Nick, call me later if you can. Otherwise, I'll leave you two to do your work."

"I'll do my best," Nick said as he grinned.

Megan closed the door and went to find Dudley.

CHAPTER 25

*A*rriving at the house, Megan opened the back door of the car. Dudley jumped out, while holding his leash in his mouth and ran toward the weeds.

As Megan walked up the steps to the front porch, Dudley ran up and joined her. She opened the front door. Dudley raced in and stopped short, the hair on his back rising. "What's up? What do you hear, boy?"

Dudley let a small growl come out of his throat, but didn't move. Megan became nervous and called out. "Hello? Is anyone here?"

"Just me," Marie said as she stepped into the hall with a dishtowel in her hands. She stopped short when she saw Dudley. "Whoa, what's that?"

"Marie, you're back from your vacation," Megan said with a smile.

"Yes, and apparently a lot has happened while I was away." She continued to stand in the hall, she and Dudley eyeing each other. "I was going to ask about the cat I found in the kitchen. At first, I thought he had wandered in, but then I saw the bed and the bowls. The size of the dog is a surprise."

Megan pet Dudley on the head. "It's okay, relax. Marie works with me."

"Tell him again so he decides he likes me," Marie said. "I'm a little nervous around dogs."

"And apparently he is around you. I think he's feeding off your body language, Marie."

"I was bitten by a dog when I was young, so they make me nervous."

Megan walked by Dudley and toward the kitchen. "Why don't we go into the kitchen. We can all sit and relax."

Dudley followed her down the hall. They entered the kitchen and Marie took one of the dog treats and offered it to Dudley. Satisfied, he took the cookie and sat down with his treat.

"When did this all happen?" Marie asked. "I'm gone for a week and things have changed."

"Well, it was a bit of a surprise for me as well, but it's not what you think."

"Tell me what's going on," Marie said as she pulled out a chair. The two sat at the table for the next twenty minutes as Megan filled her in on the events over the past couple of days.

"I'm sorry to hear about the shooting. I like the cat," Marie said. "He was very friendly when I walked in. Although he almost tripped me when he wrapped himself around my ankles."

"From what I'm told, that's what they do." Megan paused for a moment. "Hey Marie, do you have any memory of a dog living here? I don't remember one when I was growing up, but maybe when you and my father were in high school?"

Marie thought for a moment. "No, I don't remember one, but I can't say for sure."

"I realized I know nothing about pets when I agreed I would foster these two and I don't think I'd be a good pet owner. I have zero experience."

"Well, that's what life is all about. You live, and you learn," Marie said as she stood up and got ready to return to her dishes. "Many things are accomplished with no experience and perhaps we do better as a result, because we try harder."

Not knowing what to say, Megan simply nodded her head. "Well,

I'm glad you're back. I'm going to run upstairs and poke around in the attic for a bit. I need to see what kind of Christmas decorations are up there."

"Oh my, I don't remember seeing decorations on Misty Manor for at least ten years."

"We had decorations when I left for college," Megan said with a sad smile.

"Yes, but I think Rose only continued for a brief time after that and stopped. There were definitely no decorations after Hurricane Sandy, that's for sure."

"Then it's time for the tradition to start up again. We're not going to find joy in our lives unless we push it along." Megan stood up and walked toward the hall. "Are you making dinner tonight?"

"It's already in the oven," Marie said as she looked at Dudley. "But, I may have to cut an extra slice or two."

CHAPTER 26

*M*egan walked up the two flights of the grand staircase and stopped to pull out the hidden key to the lock on the attic door. Her grandmother had someone move the valuables into the attic and place a new lock on the door prior to the hurricane. Not knowing what to expect in the way of damage and looters, she didn't take any chances and Megan was glad.

Situated on a small hill, Misty Manor remained relatively safe from harm. There had been flooding around the property and the summer cottages in the back had been damaged which resulted in their being demolished this summer and offering up human remains, but that was a different story.

Megan climbed the remaining flight to the attic door and opened the padlock. She pushed the door open and stepped inside the dark room. The attic was relatively warm and ambient light filtered in through the small hexagonal windows on the side. The ceiling was at regular height, so Megan had no difficulty walking throughout the room. She reached out and turned on the lights, then walked across the floor and opened the door to the cupola to allow more light to filter into the large attic area.

Before returning to the attic, Megan took a few minutes to view the scenery from the cupola windows. She hadn't been up here since Grandma Rose died, but this room had always been her favorite as a child. Megan made herself a promise to freshen the furniture in the room and spend more time here.

She watched the December beach. The waves continued to crash the shore, but the water looked dark and cold, the sand heavy and wet. Yet the seagulls lined the beach, watching and waiting for food to come in. The rhythm of the ocean was always mesmerizing, but the water seemed less forgiving and more forceful this time of year.

Shaking off her mood, Megan walked back into the attic. She skirted various piles, searching for Christmas items. Her grandmother was an organized woman and Megan knew she would find exactly what she was looking for.

The designated Christmas area turned out to be in a corner. There were many boxes, each labeled with its contents, which were wrapped and neatly stored. Megan pulled over a chair and slowly unwrapped each box. She was looking for outdoor decorations but opened whatever lay before her. She remembered lights from ten years ago as well as wreaths and green garlands which adorned the porch handrail and posts, but didn't find any outdoor decorations in this area.

As she studied the things before her, she was drawn into the history of Christmas, especially in Misty Manor. She imagined what it must have been like to celebrate the holiday in the Grand Victorian in the early 1900s. The celebration would have been simpler with treats and decorations, the main event consisting of family around the table, enjoying great food. Perhaps turkey, sausage stuffing and roasted chestnuts.

One of the first boxes Megan unpacked held bubble lights which fascinated her as a child. She would stand by the tree, watching the bubbles move. The next box held a variety of decorations. They were lovingly packed in layers. One by one, Megan pulled out bottle brush trees in assorted colors and Putz houses. Next were free-blown Italian and vintage German glass ornaments. Some were round, and others had the classic parachute top design. Some of the glass ornaments were stenciled with scenes depicting a church in the winter, surrounded by deer and trees. Megan found hand carved wooden ornaments and crafted decorations made of pine cones with bits of holly leaves and dried berries. Next were replicas of brightly colored birds perched on small wreaths and tiny plastic Santa's dangling from gold thread. Another box was filled with beautifully painted, delicate ceramic seashells situated in individual velvet sections.

Megan found books which were all related to the holiday. There were copies of the Saturday Night Post with Christmas images and The Night Before Christmas by Little Golden Books. Megan found an old advertisement from Macy's showing a photo of Santa from the 1930s as well as an image of Father Christmas in 1925. Another layer revealed an old photo of FAO Schwartz, complete with children staring at a bounty of toys.

Continuing to explore, Megan found articles about the holiday. She learned the first National Christmas Tree was a 48-foot Balsam Fir from Vermont placed in 1923 and the first real lights on the Rockefeller Christmas Tree were placed in 1956.

She read articles about Christmas during the war. Lights weren't displayed in the early 1940s as copper was collected for WWII. Celebrations were more somber, filled with prayer for family and loved ones.

Megan continued to search through the box and learned that the television shows Rudolph the Red Nosed Reindeer, Frosty the Snowman and How the Grinch Stole Christmas were all released in the 1960s. The story of Rudolph the Red Nosed Reindeer was written by Montgomery Ward in 1939. Megan smiled to herself as she realized her tendencies as an investigative reporter must have stemmed from her grandmother's natural curiosity about life events.

Moving on she found numerous centerpieces for the dining tables, with matching runners, wall decorations, candles, and advent calendars which held a small prize for each day preceding Christmas.

Megan moved aside some of the small remaining boxes and found larger holiday items resting against the eaves in the attic. She saw a sled with ice skates hanging off the top on one side. The ocean doesn't freeze in the winter, but inland, there were many ponds, small lakes and hills that one could skate and sleigh ride on. Next, she pulled out an adorable rocking horse upon which sat dolls dressed in hand sewn dresses. Behind that was a wooden doll house filled with tiny furniture. Megan remembered seeing the doll house as a child during the holidays but not thereafter. She realized these beautiful hand-crafted toys were most likely replaced with newer plastic or technical things.

Finally, up against the wall she found several artificial Christmas trees and large wreaths. Megan sat back on her feet and thought about the decorations in the foyer. When she was very young, she had been enthralled by a tree which must have been at least fifteen feet tall. After much pleading, her grandmother had allowed her to climb several rungs up the ladder to place ornaments on the tall tree. Of course, her grandmother had stayed right behind her, holding her legs while she was there.

Megan roused herself and stood up. She replaced all the delicate ornaments in their boxes but left the area open, so she could decide what she wanted to use for this season. It was already the first week of December, so she may have to keep the indoor decorations to a minimum. She really hadn't found any outdoor decorations except for the garland and wreaths and one of the artificial trees would look lovely on the wraparound porch.

Lights from ten years ago probably wouldn't be safe to use so she decided to purchase new LED lights for the porch and windows. It would be a bit of work but would look great from the boardwalk. She vowed to talk to Teddy and Jonathan as soon as she could to get the town permit for the Boardwalk Ocean Walk, Christmas tree lighting and the fundraiser for the Hand in Paws Animal Clinic but she was hoping Nick would help her decorate.

CHAPTER 27

Megan bounded downstairs intent on formalizing her plans. Dudley heard her coming and ran to the steps, wagging his tail. Megan was glad he didn't follow her to the attic. She wasn't exactly sure what was stored up there and didn't want to take a chance of breaking anything.

As she entered the kitchen, she noticed the table was set for dinner. Dudley ran into the kitchen and stood by Marie's side. "I see the two of you have come to an understanding."

"Absolutely," Marie said as she turned around. "He understands that as long as he doesn't bite me, I'll slip him some tasty food."

Megan laughed. "You're amazing. Dudley is not going to bite you."

"Hmm, let's see," Marie said grudgingly. "Time will tell."

Megan began to comment but stopped when her cell phone started ringing. She walked out into the foyer when she answered. "Hello?"

"Megan, it's Teddy. How are you?"

"Perfect timing, I was going to call you," Megan said excitedly.

"Is everything alright?"

"Yes, it's fine," Megan said, laughing. "It's just that I spent some time going through our old Christmas decorations. I'd like you to help me arrange the Holiday Ocean Walk and tree lighting. I'm not sure if I need a permit or anything. Plus, we'll have the fundraiser for the clinic at the same time."

"We can certainly help you with that," Teddy said.

"Why did you call me?" Megan asked. "Is everything okay?"

"Yes, I wanted to give you an update. I spent the afternoon speaking with April and Carlos and we came to an agreement about salaries and such."

"They said yes? When will they start?"

"April said she can start on Thursday. She has a few things to arrange for her father beforehand. Carlos agreed to start the same day."

"I'm glad to hear that." Megan smiled as she walked about the living room.

"Of course, they'll need a week to orient to the clinic. They need to learn the layout, the clients, the books and examine the charts of the animals sheltered there."

Megan turned to see Dudley standing behind her. "When do you think they'll want the foster pets returned?" She laughed as she realized she whispered the last question.

"I think we need to give them some time before we bring everyone back," Teddy said with a sigh. "I don't want to overload them. We need them there."

"I agree," Megan said. "Did you hear anything else about Dr. Stokes and the investigation?"

"No, but the person who emptied all the meds from the safe knew what they were doing because they'll be a lot more scrutiny once April and Carlos are there."

"Very strange," Megan said. "We've got to figure out what's going on."

"And we will. Are you free for dinner Wednesday night? Perhaps you could join Jonathan, Ellen and I at the Portside? We can talk a few of these things through."

Megan paused for a moment. "That sounds lovely. I'd like that."

"Excellent," Teddy said. "I'll have Jonathan pick you up at 7:00 p.m. at Misty Manor. Is that okay?"

"Yes, absolutely. I'll see you then."

Megan hung up the phone. She'd never been to the Portside but heard it was a beautiful restaurant. Suddenly, she realized she didn't have the clothes to dress properly for dinner.

Megan pulled out her phone again and immediately dialed Georgie and Amber. She linked them on a conference call. When they were all connected she said, "Hey, what are you two doing tonight?"

"I guess it depends on why you're asking," Georgie said, laughing into the phone.

"I'm having dinner at the Portside Wednesday night and I have nothing to wear. Do you guys want to go to the mall with me?"

"You hate the mall," Amber laughed.

"I know, but I can't wear stretch pants and a t-shirt to dinner," Megan complained.

"Nick's taking you to the Portside?" Georgie asked. "What's the occasion and what bank did he rob?"

"Uh, well, it's not exactly Nick, but it's not a date either," Megan said. "It's a dinner meeting with Teddy, Ellen and his son, Jonathan."

"Teddy's son, again? I've got to see this guy," Amber said. "What are you meeting about?"

"We have to talk about the clinic and I want to ask them about the tree lighting."

"Yeah, but why do you need to go to the Portside?"

"I don't know, but Teddy invited me, so I said yes."

"Very interesting," Georgie said. "I think we'll talk more about this while we're shopping."

"Okay, Marie made dinner so after we eat, I'll come by and pick you both up."

"I'll be ready," Amber said right away.

"Wouldn't miss this for the world," Georgie said. "See you then."

CHAPTER 28

*A*fter her phone call, Megan went into the kitchen and enjoyed a delicious dinner of grilled chicken and risotto with asparagus made by Marie. Dudley and Smokey enjoyed their dinner as well, with a choice scrap added for flavor.

"I'm so glad you're back, Marie. Georgie and I pulled a few things from the upstairs rooms, so we could start to clean up Misty Manor. I had an appraiser look through the pile, but he thought it was common stuff so he's sending someone to pick it up."

"Do you mind if I look through the pile?" Marie asked while sipping her coffee.

"Absolutely not," Megan said. "Take whatever you want if you know someone who could use it."

"Thanks, I may just do that. That's very nice of you."

"Nonsense, I'm going to restore Misty Manor as soon as I can, and I need to start somewhere," Megan said. "I'm excited about bringing some joy and good memories back to the house. So, you'll be helping me out."

Marie nodded as she stood and began clearing the dishes.

"Are you okay?" Megan asked.

"Yes, I'm fine. I'm happy you're thinking about fixing up Misty

Manor. I have a lot of good memories here and it'll be nice to start making more."

"Thanks Marie. You're a big part of this plan, so pace yourself."

Marie smiled and shooed her out the door.

Megan started the car and spent a few minutes finding the right music. She was excited about shopping and looked forward to going to the mall with her friends. She drove toward the beach and down the side street toward her friend's house. Pulling over by the curb, Megan put the car in park, pulled out her phone and texted Georgie. Within minutes, both she and Amber came from the house and piled into Megan's SUV. When they were settled, she put the car in gear and headed for the mall.

"I can't believe we're actually doing this," Amber said. "The world must be coming to an end."

"Oh stop," Megan said. "What's wrong with wanting to dress a little nicer?"

"Seriously?" Georgie said with raised eyebrows.

"I am serious," Megan said. "I have to go to all these committee meetings and dinner Wednesday night. Don't forget, we have the Christmas party coming up this weekend for the Stanford Grants and you guys are invited."

"Now I need to get a new dress," Amber said as she began to preen.

"Let's not get overexcited," Megan said. "I don't know exactly who's coming but it's everyone associated with the grants. It'll probably be boring."

"Still, it's a party. It's always nice to have some food and drink in a celebratory manner," Amber said.

Megan turned to Georgie. "Given the choice, would you choose fancy Christmas party or pizza and beer?"

"That's a hard question so I won't answer it and don't put me in the middle."

Megan chuckled and parked outside the mall. Amber insisted the three of them enter through a side door, so they would be close to her favorite department store. The three women spent the next ninety minutes in the fitting room as Amber continued to pull different items off the racks and dress them appropriately.

"Did we find enough yet?" Megan complained when Amber brought in more clothes.

"I want you to have a nice assortment of dresses, suits and formal wear. You've only picked a couple of each, so we'll have to shop again after the New Year to make the most of the Spring fashions."

"Well, that's enough for now," Megan said. "It's almost Christmas. We have enough for the next few weeks."

"Hey ladies," Georgie yelled from outside their dressing room. "Want me to roll a whole rack in there for you?"

"It's not me, talk to Amber, please," Megan pleaded.

"Oh, alright," Amber said. "I swear, you two are impossible. We didn't get to the shoe department yet."

"This is further than you've ever gotten us before," Megan said. "You've got to admit that. I have a nice pair of black pumps I can wear."

"Are you sure?" Amber pouted.

"I'm positive," Megan said. "I think we've chosen enough for now."

"True," Amber said looking at their selections. "Promise me you'll come back after the New Year."

"I promise," Megan said wiggling out of a tight black skirt. "Please hand me my t-shirt."

"Sure," Amber said as she pulled up a pile of discarded clothes on the floor and started placing them on hangers. "I know teenagers who do a better job of hanging up their clothes."

Megan jumped back into her jeans and t-shirt as Amber continued to straighten the discarded clothes. Together, they put them on the rack and opened the door to find Georgie sitting on a bench. They carried their selections to the checkout counter. Megan's eyes opened when she saw the total, but before she could move, Amber added multiple discount coupons as well as points from her account and the closing price appeared to drop to half of the original.

"Is that how you do that?" Megan asked as she handed over her credit card. Teddy had placed a nice amount in her checking account, but Megan didn't want to share that with her friends.

"It's all about the sale," Amber said with a smile. "You have to look through the right racks."

"Okay, well I pulled you guys out here, so I'll buy."

"Buy what?" Georgie asked.

"Whatever you want," Megan said. "You guys name it. Ice cream, coffee or liquor? It's all here."

"I don't know about you ladies, but I have to go to work tomorrow so no alcohol for me," Amber said. "Besides, I don't have many calories left to use today."

Georgie rolled her eyes upward. "Whatever, how about if we just get coffee?"

"Sounds good to me," Megan said as the three trailed out of the store and into the main mall. They walked toward center court, into the coffee shop, up to the counter and studied the menu. "I'd like a decaf latte."

"Me too," Georgie said. "The cinnamon buns smell great."

"Make mine an ultra-skinny," Amber said.

After ordering and waiting for their coffee, they took a seat at a nearby table to talk. Shoppers, carrying decorated holiday bags, walked by them full of the Christmas spirit as they listened to the holiday songs and laughed. They wore freshly decorated Santa hats, jingle bells and wool sweaters.

Megan watched as several teenagers walked into a pet store across the way. They browsed and eventually came out into the main mall with their purchases. Megan took a sip of coffee as she verbalized her thoughts.

"So why would you go to a pet store in a mall instead of an animal shelter or clinic?

Her friends thought for a moment and then offered some suggestions. "Convenience, hands down," Amber said. "Plus, the merchandise is usually much prettier."

Georgie leaned forward. "I hope they don't have animals in there. I would hate to think they're running a puppy mill."

"No, I don't see any animals or cages," Megan said as she studied the store.

"The things you buy at a shelter are usually very functional. Also, they have sales at the mall, which is very important," Amber said, pleased with herself. "I've seen lovely collars and clothes for pets in the mall. On the other hand, I would never buy their food here. I think the better discount would be one of those mega pet stores."

"That's exactly the point," Georgie said. "A pet store is trying to make money and a pet shelter or clinic is about saving animal's lives and preventing cruelty."

"Don't delude yourself," Amber said. "Even shelters will euthanize pets that aren't adopted. Every adoption opens more space in a shelter for another animal in need."

"The conditions in these pet stores aren't always stellar," Georgie said, picking up her cup.

Megan was thoughtful. "I guess that's why Grandma Rose insisted the Hand in Paws clinic be a no-kill shelter. Teddy was discussing some local ordinances that limit where pet stores can get their animals." Megan drained her coffee cup. "I have to admit, I never really thought much about it before."

"Well, if you're going to be the director or board chair or whatever big cheese position you're supposed to take, I guess you're going to have to think about it, a lot," said Amber.

"You're right about that. I keep saying I have a lot to learn."

"Okay, enough talking ladies," Amber said as she drained her ultra-skinny latte. "Let's get these clothes home and hung before they start to wrinkle." She threw her cup in the garbage and helped carry Megan's new purchases to the car.

CHAPTER 29

*J*ared looked around the small kitchen. Everything looked yellow. The walls were painted mustard yellow. The plastic over the tablecloth was yellowed from age. The dingy Formica counters looked yellow as well as the curtains at the window over the sink.

Jared turned on the water and grabbed a piece of paper towel. Wetting the towel, he brushed it over his forehead to wipe away the sweat. Earlier, he felt lightheaded and dizzy. Now he felt nauseous as well. His neck was throbbing, and pain was seeping down into his left arm and chest.

"Finally, you show up," Micky said as he walked into the kitchen.

"I'm not feeling too good," he said. "I think I'm gonna heave."

"Then go out the back door. The last thing I need is puke covering the floors."

Jared sat for a moment and waited for the wave of dizziness to end. "I didn't see a doctor, and now I feel horrible. Micky, do you have any extra antibiotics here? Were there any in the meds I took?"

"I don't know," Micky said. "But even if there was, it's for the business. You'd better get something fast because we still have two dogs to deliver before Christmas. You know what we're looking for. Those two pure bred dogs they scheduled to be boarded. We have to snatch them as soon as possible, before the people at the clinic have enough time to fix all the cameras."

"How are we gonna explain that?"

"We're not. As soon as we grab those two dogs, we can lay low for a bit. You disappear. The clinic takes the heat. Besides, the big boss has been looking at another place. This one's getting too hot."

"I don't know, Micky."

Micky sat down in the opposite chair. "Hey, don't make me slap you and definitely don't make me go into the clinic. I'm allergic to those damn animals. I don't want to have to grab them."

"I'll do the best I can, but those dogs ain't coming in for another couple days and I'm definitely not feeling too good. I've got to get some antibiotics."

Micky got up and went into the cabinet. A few minutes later he slapped a bottle of aspirin on the table. "Here, take some of these. It'll get rid of the fever and take some of the swelling down."

Jared shook four aspirin out of the bottle and swallowed them dry. "I hope this works."

"I do too," Micky said. "One more job and then we can take a break."

"Okay, you got it, Micky." Jared crossed his arms on the table, put his head down and promptly fell asleep.

CHAPTER 30

"Hurry," Amber said. "You're going to be late."

"It's 4:00 p.m.," Megan said. "Jonathan will be here at 7:00 p.m."

"Exactly, we're running out of time." Amber pulled Megan toward the bathroom and handed her a few bottles of shampoo and conditioner as well as a razor and other creams. "Hurry up. Wash your hair and don't forget to shave."

"It's not like I've been in the woods for the last three months," Megan said with a scowl as Georgie walked into the room.

"It's hard to tell. This is a special night and you need some help. When you get out of the shower, we'll pluck your eyebrows and start with your moisturizer while we do your hair." Amber looked at her watch while Georgie snickered behind her. "C'mon, Megan. Go shower. I'll plug in the hair dryer."

Amber shoved a pile of towels into Megan's arms and pushed her toward the bathroom. When Megan closed the door, and turned the water on, Amber shook her head at Georgie. "I swear I didn't work this hard getting us all ready for the prom."

Georgie laughed. "Back then we only needed fifteen minutes to get the same result an hour takes today."

"And that's only with cooperation," Amber said as she pulled a chair over to a makeshift makeup table and plugged in the hair dryer. She assembled an array of moisturizers, foundation, blush, eye shadow, liners and other products."

"Are you sure Megan wants to be this made up?" Georgie asked looking over the makeup.

"I don't know, but she's feeling like she has to take the next step since she asked us about clothes shopping. She's worn nothing but jeans, stretch pants and t-shirts since she came home. It's okay to push her along a bit. We'll help her step up her wardrobe and style her hair just to see the possibilities. She won't wear makeup otherwise," Amber said as she sat on the side of the bed and waited for Megan to emerge from the bathroom. "Besides, I can't wait to see this new guy, Jonathan. A few of the girls have noticed him around town and they say he's a real catch."

"What if Megan doesn't want to be caught?"

"She doesn't have to be, but let her go out to a fancy dinner and feel beautiful for a night. She's been so down in the dumps since Grandma Rose died. Maybe this will lift her spirits a little."

"What about Nick?"

"What about him? I love the guy and he's a hunk now as well. He looks damn good in uniform, but lately he's been busy with work and a bit remiss with Megan. I don't know, maybe he's just giving her space or waiting until she comes out of her funk, but it certainly wouldn't hurt for him to step it up a bit, too. Anyway, as her friends, we're just concentrating on her and the guys will have to worry about their own issues."

"I agree," Georgie said as she sat on the floor and scratched Dudley behind the ears. She leaned forward and nuzzled his head with her own. He licked her chin while she laughed and hugged the dog to her. He wagged his tail as Smokey cuddled up and joined in the embrace. "I was hoping Dudley would grow on her."

"He hasn't?" Amber said as she watched the group on the floor.

"I think her head is spinning and she doesn't know what to address first," Georgie said. "I helped her clean some of the bedrooms on the third floor. I know she wants to restore Misty Manor and open all the rooms. She was beginning to focus on that project when this whole Hand in Paws business started up. I hope they catch the jerk soon. These poor animals."

"I don't know about that," Amber said. "I think most of the animals that were emergently fostered are getting a better deal than if they were still in cages in the clinic. I know we talked about having the fundraiser for the Hand in Paws clinic at the Christmas tree lighting, but I would love to get the rest of the animals adopted before Christmas."

"One step at a time," Georgie said. "As you said, let's work on Megan and then we'll conquer the world."

Both women looked up when they heard the door to the bathroom open. Megan stepped into the bedroom wearing a bathrobe and a towel wrapped around her head. "Okay, I'm done with my shower."

"Great, now step over here and sit down," Amber said as she guided Megan toward the makeup table. Amber opened a jar and gave Megan instructions on how to apply the cream. She then took the towel off Megan's head and began to brush, and blow dry her hair. While her hair was pinned, Amber finished applying Megan's makeup.

While they worked, Georgie stayed on the floor and played with Dudley and Smokey. The women laughed and talked while they got Megan ready for dinner. They chatted about the Stanford Grant Christmas party and what they would wear and possibly eat for dinner. "So, this is practice for Saturday night," Amber said as she unpinned Megan's hair and began to brush it forward. She grabbed the curling iron and set curls throughout. While they primped they talked about Christmas traditions from their years in high school and made an agreement to practice more of them next year.

They discussed ideas for the tree lighting and the fundraiser. Amber said she would make final plans with Tommy, so the band could play at town square when the tree was lit, and Megan made it a point to discuss permits with Teddy and Jonathan at dinner. Megan also pointed out that others on the committee were excited about working together.

Once the makeup was done, Amber went to the closet and selected a cranberry sheath dress with a matching Burberry wrap. "You're going to look great in this dress."

"I don't know about that. I'm not in decent shape anymore."

"You don't work out, but you've got a beautiful figure," Amber said. "Besides, you don't need large muscles."

"There's nothing wrong with being in good shape," Georgie said to the group.

"Of course not," Amber said as she took the dress off the hanger.

Megan donned the clothes and twirled in front of her friends.

"You look beautiful," Georgie said as she watched her friend.

"I feel very strange," Megan said laughing. "I'm not used to makeup or fancy clothes."

"It's just one dinner and one Christmas party," Amber said. "It is absolutely okay to feel special for a night so enjoy it."

"Thank you," Megan said as she looked in the mirror once again to make sure the image she saw was really her.

CHAPTER 31

*D*avis growled as he sat at his desk. He looked through the pile of papers which sat before him and reread each narrative about the investigation. He knew there was something he was missing. This shooting was more than an average violation. There had to be a bigger connection. Davis looked up when Nick walked into the precinct and straight into his office.

"You got something?" Davis asked.

"I don't know," Nick said. "I've been looking at the volunteers. There are five of them that show up at multiple animal clinics or shelters. Coincidentally, all four shelters have been hit or robbed in some fashion."

"Interesting," Davis said as he reviewed the lists. "Who are they?"

"A couple of females who work for a company that has a very strong philanthropic philosophy and from a look in their file, I don't see anything suspicious. Then there's Judy Bowan. She's recently the head of the volunteers at the Hand in Paws clinic and admits to working in a couple of other shelters. There are two other volunteers that have worked at various animal clinics but they're in and out and their files show no other volunteer work. I'm trying to run them down. What else have we got?"

"Not a lot at this point. The veterinarian is still in a coma. They ran the bullet through forensics and it was clean for prints. We got a ton of fingerprints at the scene, but they match everyone who says they're supposed to be there. Theodore Harrison Carter is the attorney for the grant. He gave us a good bit of information about the clinic but nothing that helps identify anyone."

"What about the board members?"

"They're all town citizens who have lived here or been on various committees for years, well known to the community. The only unknown in that grouping is Jonathan Brandon Carter, son of Theodore," Davis said as he handed Nick a document.

"What do we know about him?" Nick asked as he looked over the paper Davis had just handed him.

"Not a lot. We tracked his passport. He came here from London a couple of months ago. He was raised in England by his natural mother who is deceased. He studied some sort of law at Princeton with extra study at Oxford University. Ivy League all the way. He's either had or has a position there but is now in New Jersey spending time with his father. We have no idea why."

"He was at the emergency meeting for the Hand in Paws clinic the other night," Nick said. "He had a few suggestions about issues, but I have no idea what his official position is. I'll have to check him out before he gets himself too comfortable."

"You do that, Junior," Davis said as he raised his eyebrows in a questioning glance. "How about the patrons?"

"There's quite a few, but no patterns I can see. They're regular customers of the shelter. They either come in and buy food and supplies or drop off donations for the other animals in the shelter. Many people use the clinic as their veterinarian so the animals who come in are their regular patients. I didn't see any particular pattern of people that visited the clinics on the day of the robberies."

"We'll have to keep watching until someone makes a mistake."

"We've got eyes on the clinic," Nick said as he threw all the paper-work back on the desk. "Beyond that, I've got nothing."

CHAPTER 32

"He's going to be here soon," Amber said as she finished off Megan's hair with what seemed to be a whole bottle of hair spray. Next, she picked up a bottle of perfume and lightly applied the scent to Megan. "Okay, it's 6:55 p.m. Now we wait."

"Shouldn't we go downstairs?" Megan asked.

"Marie is down there, isn't she?"

"Yes," Megan replied.

"Then let her get the door. She'll call us and then we'll go downstairs. Never be ready the second a guy gets to the house."

"Amber, you realize this isn't a date, right?" Megan asked again.

"It doesn't matter what it is. You're going to a beautiful dinner and you'll feel better if you look good."

Suddenly, they heard the doorbell echoed by Dudley barking as he raced to the front door.

"I'll get it," Marie said as she made her way from the kitchen through the foyer.

Amber pulled Georgie and Megan along the hall and down one flight of stairs to the second floor. They stayed at the end of the landing where they could watch the activities in the foyer below without being seen.

After looking through the peep hole, Marie opened the front door and beckoned for the visitor to come inside. She held her hand out to Dudley to make sure the dog did not jump on their guest. Jonathan stepped over the threshold and into the foyer, carrying a dozen roses. He was dressed in a designer midnight blue suit that nicely set off his blond hair.

"Wowza," Amber said as they watched him shake hands with Marie and introduce himself. She turned to Megan. "Wait until Marie calls you."

"I second that thought," Georgie whispered to the group. "He is quite dreamy."

"Now, I'm nervous," Megan whispered back.

"Just go now then," Amber whispered and pushed Megan further out on the landing in view of Marie and Jonathan.

Marie looked up and said, "Oh Megan, I was just going to call you. Jonathan is here."

"I'm coming down," Megan said as she began the final flight down the grand staircase. When she reached the bottom, Dudley ran over to greet her as she walked toward her guest.

"You look gorgeous," Jonathan said as he handed her the roses. "These are for you."

"Thank you. They're beautiful," Megan said as she took the roses. "That's so sweet of you, Jonathan."

"American beauties for an American beauty." Jonathan smiled broadly at Megan as she realized her heart was starting to pound in her chest.

Upstairs, Amber elbowed Georgie who almost yelped out loud.

"Don't do that," Georgie said as she rubbed her ribcage.

"Would you like me to put those in water for you?" Marie asked as she held her arms out toward Megan.

"Please," Megan said as she handed the floral bouquet to Marie.

"Shall we go?" Jonathan asked as he held his arm out to Megan.

"Of course." Megan looped her arm through Jonathan's. She turned back to Marie. "I won't be home too late and thanks for watching Dudley for me."

"Don't worry about us. Enjoy yourselves," Marie said as she escorted them to the front door.

"It was delightful to meet you," Jonathan said before they left the house. He held Megan's arm as they walked down the front porch stairs and to his car in the driveway. He held the passenger door open for her as she slipped into his Jaguar coupe. "Watch your arm," he said as he gently closed the door, then walked around the car. Jonathan opened his door and got in the driver's seat. The car whispered as he started it up, placed it in gear and headed toward Main Street.

"You look quite lovely tonight," Jonathan said as he smiled at Megan to make conversation.

"Thank you, once again," Megan said, nervously shifting in the Jaguar. She liked his English accent when he spoke. "It was so nice of you to pick me up."

"My pleasure," Jonathan said. "I've only been in town a few months so let me know if I'm heading in the right direction."

"Looks right so far," Megan said too quickly. She realized her nerves made her voice sound high and tinny. "You have a lovely car."

"Thanks, I would have put on the seat warmers but it's not that cold for December. Unless you want me to put yours on."

"No, I'm fine," Megan said. "You're right. It's been a mild December. What's December like in London?"

"The weather is not very nice in London during December. It's a bit strange because the center of London is much warmer than other areas, so snow rarely sticks to the ground. Sometimes, we have snow in January, but nothing more than a dusting in December."

"We don't have a lot of snow at the beach either," Megan said. "The winters at the ocean can be warm or they can be very cold."

"London is cold in December. The temp stays around forty degrees and it rains a lot. That's Fahrenheit for you, but 4 degrees Celsius for us," Jonathan clarified. "The worst thing is we only have about three hours of daylight."

"That sounds awful," Megan said. "Especially when you're used to living by the beach."

"Agreed, but then it's like everyone's hometown. There are things you hate and things you come to love which you can't find anywhere else."

"Point taken," Megan said.

"I hear many people love the restaurant we're going to."

"I don't really know. I've never been to the Portside, but I've heard it's very nice."

"You're about to find out," Jonathan said as he pulled the car into the valet line. They waited for a few moments until the valet approached the car and opened the doors for them. Megan waited on the sidewalk until Jonathan came around to join her. Once again, taking her arm, he led her into the stylish lobby of the restaurant. Megan noted it was decorated with marble and lit with crystal chandeliers. Palm trees highlighted the front corners and holiday bunting was hung throughout the room. Wreaths twinkled with white lights as fresh bouquets of poinsettias, pine cones and fragrant white carnations sat on side tables. Piano music was playing softly in the background.

The pair approached a hostess station and Jonathan gave his name. The hostess turned and beckoned to the maître d' who immediately responded. "Good evening, Mr. Carter. It's nice to see you again."

"Thank you, James, we're here to meet my father."

"Of course, they're already here," he said offering a warm smile. "Please, follow me." They followed as he escorted them to a round table near the back. Overhead was a lovely sconce decorated for the holiday. Megan sat when the maître d' pulled out her chair. Jonathan waited for her to be seated before he took his own seat. When the maître d' left to offer some privacy, Jonathan greeted his father and his companion, Ellen. They in turn greeted Megan and voiced how excited they were to have this intimate dinner. The four chatted for several minutes before James returned and asked if he could offer them a drink.

Deferring to Teddy, he asked for wine to be brought to the table. "Excellent, sir," James said as he left to summon the sommelier. James returned and recited the specials of the day with suggestions as he emphasized the talents of the culinary team. He noted the Chef de cuisine had specific recommendations for the party but as he was unavailable, the Sous-chef came to the table to discuss their food choices. He offered many delectable dishes, but they finally decided on Beef Wellington with multiple layers of pate and mushrooms as well as a Saffron Fregola with Seafood, Herb braised lamb shanks, and blue cheese lobster beignets.

Within minutes, the sommelier approached the table, wearing his tastevin on a silk ribbon around his neck. He suggested several wines that would pair nicely with their food choices and waited for them to make their final decisions upon which he bowed and walked away to direct the servers. Within minutes, a server returned and poured champagne into flutes for each one of them. When he was done, he left the table. Teddy picked up the glass and held it aloft until everyone had raised their glass. "To Rose and her lovely granddaughter, Megan."

The group all clinked glasses and sipped the champagne. "This is delicious," Megan said as she placed her glass back on the table.

Teddy turned to Megan and placed his hand on her arm. "I've been wanting to have this dinner for quite a while, but it never seemed appropriate since you've returned. We've all been mourning the loss of our dear Rose and then all that ugly business with your father, Dean."

Megan looked sad for a moment and then smiled. "Well, this is very lovely, Teddy. Thank you for arranging this dinner." Megan looked at her table companions as well as the room. "The company as well as the ambience is very special."

"Having my son here as well as the Christmas Season makes it all the nicer," Teddy said as he beamed and took Ellen's hand.

"I don't remember a time when Teddy was so happy," Ellen said as she squeezed his hand.

"I'm glad you feel that way," Jonathan said as he smiled at his father and Megan.

"Unfortunately, we need to have some banal discussion before our dinner is served. Let's get that out of the way quickly." The table quieted and let him speak. "Dr. May, or April as we'll call her, will be starting in the clinic tomorrow. Carlos will be with her and hopefully their presence will deter any further criminal activity."

"Have they discovered anything yet?" Megan asked, while silently thinking to herself that she hadn't heard from Nick in a day or so. For a moment, she imagined herself at home with him eating pizza in the kitchen.

"Nothing, as far as I know," Teddy replied. "They're investigating many people and asking for a lot of information about the grant. When you're ready, we'll begin your lessons regarding Rose's estate. I would like to have Jonathan with us for those discussions as he will be your official liaison."

"Of course," Megan said as her stomach clenched for unknown reasons.

"And I understand you have a specific issue you'd like to discuss tonight," Teddy said as he looked at Megan.

Megan blinked for a moment and was at a loss for words until she realized what Teddy was referring to. "Yes, I'd like to ask for help arranging whatever needs to be done to officially reinstate the Ocean Holiday Walk as well as the Christmas tree lighting in the town square. I know there are only a few weeks left until Christmas, but I'd like to incorporate the fundraiser for the Hand in Paws Animal Clinic. The first goal would be to raise money for a non-profit organization, but the main goal would be to raise awareness of the needs of the animals. I just don't know what I need to do."

Teddy stared at Megan, speechless for a few moments and tears glistened in his eyes.

"What?" Megan asked, suddenly frightened she had made a major mistake.

Teddy swallowed hard and shook his head. "You have no idea how much you look and sound like your grandmother. For a moment, I was back to one of the first dinners I had with her. I so wish she could be here, but I know she is watching from above and is so proud of you."

Seeing the tears in Teddy's eyes set off Megan as she thought of Rose and how much she missed her. She could barely whisper as tears dropped down her cheeks. "I have no idea what I'm doing. I'm just trying to accomplish what seems to be right and make sense."

"My dear, that is exactly why your grandmother was so successful," Teddy said as he smiled at her.

Jonathan slid his chair closer to Megan and wrapped his arms around her. She buried her head in his shoulder and let more tears loose. He stroked her back and whispered in her hair. Teddy reached over and squeezed her arm again. "I didn't mean to upset you, Megan. I simply wanted you to know how proud we all are of you."

Megan nodded against Jonathan's shoulder as he took out his handkerchief and wiped her tears. The maître d' approached with several servers behind him, but paused as he realized something was amiss. Teddy noticed him and waved him over to the table. They served chilled salads and fresh bread to each of them. James asked each if they wanted ground pepper or cheese on their salad. Jonathan pulled away from Megan who quickly composed herself. After waiting a few minutes, she was able to finish the delicious salad and finish her champagne even though her hand shook at first.

When all four were done with their salad, the servers returned and cleared the table of their dishes. One of the servers swept the linen tablecloth and reset their places with clean silverware and fresh napkins. The group leaned back against their chairs until they were done.

Within minutes the servers returned with their entrees and waited until the maître d' returned to the table. He lifted the silver lid from the first entrée and checked the dish. Satisfied, he served it to Megan who waited until all were served. One by one, he checked the meals for their presentation and temperature before approving. He then waved the servers away and said, "Please try your entries and let me know if it is to your liking."

Each one of them picked up the proper fork and tasted their food. Nodding their approval, the maître d' smiled, bowed and walked away.

"This is absolutely delicious," Megan said as she smiled at the group. "I've never had Beef Wellington before."

"The lobster is grand as well," Ellen said as she tasted a bit of the beignet.

"Excellent restaurant and presentation," Jonathan said as he obviously approved of the meal.

"I knew you'd all be happy," Teddy said as he placed his fork on his plate. "I'm so happy you were able to join us, and I hope we have the opportunity to do this more often. I'm looking forward to a wonderful relationship."

The group continued to enjoy their meal as they passed small talk about the holiday, the weather and the beach. Eventually, the conversation turned back to what they would need to do to ensure the Ocean Holiday Walk and tree lighting. "I can't imagine there will be much of a problem. However, we'll have to hurry with preparation. We must arrange delivery of a tree, have it decorated and ready for the lighting. Of course, we have to check on insurance in case it falls over."

"Why don't we have the town decorate it?" Megan suggested. "We can hang a few ornaments but when we advertise the tree lighting, why don't we suggest every family bring a homemade ornament to add to the tree?"

"Great idea," Jonathan said. "I think the children will love it. The only problem is that we're going to be restricted with advertising time. We'll have to rely on word of mouth to get us through."

"Now may be the perfect time to use social media to spread the word. I'm sure the town has a website or perhaps a social media page we can use. Maybe we can hang a few signs around town and I'm sure my friends can help me get the word out," Megan said, excitement building in her voice.

"I'll go to town hall tomorrow and begin to fill out the forms. I'll have to check the calendar to make sure there are no other events scheduled in town square," Ellen said. "And then I can appeal to the event coordinators." She turned to Megan. "I'll call you as soon as I leave the building."

"Thank you, I'll be nervous until I hear something," Megan said with a smile.

James returned to the table and began to tell them about the offerings on the desert table. They had a choice of Crème brûlée, chocolate mousse, white chocolate cheesecake, Tiramisu and a Torte. After discussing how they shouldn't have any more to eat, they each choose a dessert and ordered coffee as well, then passed the time discussing more arrangements for the celebration. They refused the offer of cognac or brandy after dessert by declaring they couldn't fit another bite.

"Well, we should be off," Jonathan said as he could see Megan was becoming restless. He stood up and pulled out Megan's chair for her. He took her hand as she stood and gathered her purse. Teddy and Ellen also stood and the four of them said goodbye with hugs, handshakes and a promise to speak again the next day.

Jonathan led Megan out to the lobby and handed his ticket over to the valet who scrambled to bring the Jaguar to the front door immediately. They each had their doors opened for them and they climbed in and secured themselves before the valet closed the doors, but not before receiving a generous tip from Jonathan.

Jonathan put the car in gear and drove away.

"Do you mind if I open the window a little bit?" Megan asked as she turned toward Jonathan.

"Of course not. Are you feeling alright?" He continued to drive down Ocean Ave.

"Yes, I'm fine. I know it's dark and I can't see the surf from the car, but I always like to listen to it as I pass. Somehow, it's comforting to know the ocean's always out there, day or night."

"Very rhythmic and soothing," Jonathan said. "Would you like to stop?"

Megan shivered, not sure if it was the crisp temperature or being alone with Jonathan. He was so handsome, polite and available. She was nervous.

"Not tonight, but thank you for asking."

"It was a lovely dinner and it was nice being with my father. I feel like I've lost time with him, especially with mum gone, but I've got a beautiful family in London as well."

"That's very special, Jonathan. I'm glad for you."

They reached Misty Manor and pulled into the large driveway. Jonathan walked around the car and opened the door for Megan. Once again, he reached out and took her hand as he helped her out of the car. With his hand at her back, they walked to the front door of Misty Manor.

Megan had her key in her hand, but paused as she knew Dudley was on the other side of the door. "I think I should say goodnight here. I don't want the dog jumping on you at this time of night."

"If you wish, but I'll wait until I see you inside." Jonathan took her hands and kissed her lightly on the cheek. She took in the scent of his fragrant cologne. "I hope we can do this again soon and not for any committee reasons."

Megan smiled. "I would like that, Jonathan. It was a lovely evening."

He smiled back and squeezed her hands. "Then off with you. I'm not leaving this porch until the front door has closed behind you." He dropped her hands and she unlocked the door.

Megan slipped inside but waved as she turned. "Goodnight Jonathan." Closing the door, she leaned back on it and took a deep breath while Dudley ran up to her and nuzzled her hand. She knelt to pet him, and he licked her face and nuzzled her shoulder.

"I'm here, it's all okay," Megan said as she scratched him behind the ears. Behind him, Smokey slowly sauntered up to the front door and rubbed against them as they hugged.

CHAPTER 33

The next morning, Megan awoke to a peculiar sound on her bed. She was lying on her side facing the window with Dudley curled up against her back. Smokey was stretched out on the lower part of the bed and was kneading the blanket with his claws while purring, an occasional nail getting caught in the fabric.

Not sure if it was due to wine, food or company, Megan had difficulty falling asleep the night before. It really had been a wonderful evening but so unlike anything she was ever used to. She had tossed and turned, reviewing conversation in her head until early in the morning when she finally dropped off into a deep sleep.

"Everybody off the bed." Once the animals jumped off, Megan got up and readied for the day. She arrived downstairs to find Marie had stayed overnight, but was already up and keeping company with the animals.

"They ran in here like they were starving. I fed them, but I didn't bring the dog outside," Marie said as she handed Megan a steaming cup of coffee. "I'll leave that to you."

"Thanks, we all appreciate it," Megan said with a sigh as she tasted the coffee.

"Looks like you had a late night. Would you like me to fix you some breakfast?"

"No thanks, I'm still full from dinner last night."

"I've heard the Portside is some fancy restaurant."

"Then you've heard right," Megan said as she sipped her coffee. "It was some meal."

"Mighty handsome gentleman," Marie said as tilted her head and wiped down the counter.

"Yes, Jonathan is very handsome." Megan was grateful Marie didn't ask all the questions that must be churning within her as Megan wasn't sure she had any answers herself.

"Will you be home for dinner tonight?"

"I don't think so," Megan said. "I promised the girls we'd get together for a pizza." She placed her coffee on the table and shook her head. "But thank you, anyway. There's always too much food around the holidays."

"I'm sure our friends here will want to eat."

Megan laughed as she placed his cup on the counter. "I'm going to run up to the clinic to welcome April to her new position."

"Are you taking you know who with you?" Marie asked as she nodded toward the dog.

"Yes, I usually do because I don't want him to forget the building for when things go back to normal. I think he likes seeing all his old friends."

"The cat and I can hang out and clean the litter box today," Marie said with a grin.

Megan stopped and gave the woman a big hug. "I'm sorry, Marie. I feel like I dump so much on you."

"No problem," Marie said with a laugh. "I love Misty Manor and I love being here, so I'm very happy. I like the cat. Now go."

Megan walked into the foyer, picked up her bag, and whistled to Dudley. He came running and the two of them went out the front door. After visiting the weeds, Dudley ran to the back seat of the car and hopped in. When he was settled, Megan drove to the animal clinic.

Together they walked through the back door and found April looking through some papers. She was wearing a white starched coat with instruments in a pocket.

"Hi, how are you?" Megan asked when April looked up.

April smiled and said, "Truth be told, I'm a little nervous. The average animal I'm used to treating is about one thousand pounds. Either a horse or a cow. These tiny furry creatures are so precious, I'm afraid I'll break one."

Megan laughed. "I doubt that very much. You'll be fine, and you have Carlos to help you as well."

"We haven't spent much time together, but he seems very nice."

"I'm sure," Megan said looking around. "Was everything okay when you came in this morning?"

"I think so," April said. "Nothing seemed to be disturbed and the animals were quiet. Of course, I have no idea what animals were here last night, but I plan to have a complete list of names when I leave tonight. By the end of the week, I'll make sure each one of our guests are chipped and registered as well."

The two women turned when they heard a noise behind them. Carlos walked into the room and a few minutes later he was followed by Nick.

"Hi Carlos. Nick, what are you doing here?" Megan asked.

"I might ask you the same thing," Nick said as Carlos nodded to her with a smile.

"I came to make sure April felt comfortable. I wanted to make sure she didn't need any help with orientation. And you?"

"I wanted the same thing," Nick said coldly. "Teddy told me a shipment of opioids will be arriving today, and I want to be sure they're securely locked away, so we don't have any trouble."

"I'll be on the lookout," Carlos said. "No one will get by me."

"I'm glad to hear that. I don't want any more trouble in the clinic, either," Megan said as she looked at Carlos.

"None of us do," April said. "We're watching everything and everyone right now."

No one spoke for a moment, so Megan picked up Dudley's leash.

"Okay, well I guess I'll be going. April, please call me if you have any questions. I mean, technically Teddy is going to take care of all your paperwork, but I just wanted to let you know I'm here for you if you need anything."

"I appreciate it, Megan." April smiled as she spoke.

Turning toward the door, Megan was surprised to find Judy Bowan standing right behind her. She jumped back before knocking the woman over. "Sorry, I didn't see you there."

"No problem, Dearie. I just came back here to tell our new doctor there are a few customers out front and I'm not sure how she wants us to handle things."

"Are they upset?" Megan asked.

"No, I think one woman brought her cat in for vomiting and there's another person looking for special dog food." Judy turned to April. "I can get it out of the supply closet for you if you want or would you like to speak to them first?"

"Is there anyone else in the front room right now?" Nick asked.

"Oh sure," Judy said, showing her dimples. "Two of our volunteers. They're cleaning the cages and feeding the animals."

April walked toward Judy and ushered her back toward the front. "C'mon, I'll speak to the customers about their questions. Does the cat lady want an official visit? Then she should register with the receptionist first."

"Gee, I'm not really sure," Judy said, dimples popping out.

"Well, let's go find out," April said with a smile as she turned toward the front. "I'll talk to you all later."

"I should follow them to make sure they don't need any help," Carlos said with a nod. "Have a nice day."

Nick and Megan were left alone in the back room, but neither spoke for a minute. Nick appeared very tense with a large frown on his face.

Megan broke the silence first. "Are you alright?"

"Yea, I'm fine," Nick said stiffly, shifting his weight and crossing his arms.

"You don't sound fine," Megan replied. "What's up?"

"Nothing new," he said shaking his head. "And you?"

"Nothing exciting," Megan said, confused at his attitude. "Have you found anything new about the clinic?"

"Not much, but we have our suspicions."

"Anything you'd care to share?" Megan tried again.

"Not really," Nick said as she shoved his hands into his jeans.

"Okay." After an awkward moment of silence, Megan gathered Dudley's leash. "I'll leave you to it then and go." Megan shook her head and began to lead Dudley to the door.

Just as she got there, Nick called after her. "I called you last night."

Meagan turned around. "I didn't get a message."

"You didn't answer your phone," Nick pouted.

"I didn't hear it," Megan said defensively. "What time did you call?"

"Fairly early in the evening. To be honest, I went over to Misty Manor, but Marie said you weren't there."

"That's right," Megan said. "I had a business dinner."

"So, I hear," Nick mumbled when he turned around.

Megan walked over to face him. "What is that supposed to mean?"

"I heard you were at the Portside last night."

"I was, it's no secret. You have friends spying on me or what?"

"I heard it was a mighty cozy looking group." Nick said with a frown.

"What exactly are you trying to say, Nick? I was at the Portside talking to Teddy, Ellen and Jonathan about getting permits or whatever we need to do to have the Ocean walk and the tree lighting. Tommy already said his band can play for us, but we have a lot to do very quickly to make all the arrangements. Do you have a problem with that?"

"No," Nick said quietly. "I was just surprised to hear it from someone else."

"Oh, I needed permission? I haven't heard much from you lately and when you do call me, I can tell you're not being honest. And who's spying on me anyway?" Sensing her tension, Dudley began to nuzzle her hand from her side.

"No one is spying," Nick said. "I meant to call but I've been busy with this case."

"Yes, in a very weird way," Megan said. "You're just hanging around. What's that all about? I've never seen an investigation handled this way."

"There's a lot more to it than you know," Nick admitted.

"And that's exactly my point," Megan said. "I'm supposed to oversee the damn place, and everyone is keeping me out of the loop. Are you planning on living here until something happens?"

"No, there's other people in place."

"Like who?"

"I'm not at liberty to say," Nick said with a shrug.

"Once again, thank you for making my point. I guess I'd better go now." Megan tugged on Dudley's leash and they walked out the back door.

CHAPTER 34

"*I* can't believe the nerve of him," Megan said to herself in the car. She traveled down Main Street and stopped at a red light when her phone began to ring. Checking the car display and recognizing the number, Megan pushed the button to connect. "Hello?"

"Hey, it's Georgie, how are you?"

"I just saw Nick," Megan said. "He makes me so mad."

"Oh, trouble in paradise?"

"Some paradise. Are we still meeting for pizza tonight?"

"Of course, you'd better be meeting us. We want to hear everything about last night."

"Why not? Apparently, everyone else has."

"What's that supposed to mean?"

"I'll explain later. What time and where?" Megan asked.

"Considering your mood, we should probably order in. Let's meet at Amber's house at 6:00 p.m."

"Sounds good to me," Megan said. She knew it was difficult for Georgie to host friends since she still lived with her mom in a small house near the beach. Georgie had been promoted in her lifeguard duties and hadn't yet met the man of her dreams, so the arrangement was still convenient for her and her mother.

"I'll call Amber to let her know," Georgie said.

"If there's any problem we can all meet at my place," Megan said. "The only other person there is Marie, so we'll have privacy."

"Okay, I'll ask Amber and let you know."

"Text me," Megan said. "I have a few errands to run and I don't want to miss your call."

"You got it. See you later."

Megan reached forward and hit the red button to disconnect the call in the car. She headed west as she wanted to see an old friend of hers. During the night she had an idea pop into her head and she wanted to see if it would pan out before she told anyone else about it.

Traveling along Route 34 and then County Road 537, she finally came to her destination. She turned into a long dirt road which wound down and around a beautiful horse farm.

Megan had received a card from one of her old high school friends when Grandma Rose passed away. Her friend had expressed her condolences and asked Megan to drop in whenever she could, highlighting her phone and address on the card. Megan had called the number to thank her and the two had an enjoyable conversation through which Megan found out her friend was now boarding horses and growing Christmas trees on the back of a farm. Knowing she would have to work quickly if the permits were obtained to find and have a tree delivered for the town square, Megan wanted to see if her friend would be able to help.

Pulling up in front of the farmhouse, Megan turned off the ignition and got out of the car. She told Dudley to stay put and left a window open a few inches. She didn't see anyone from the driveway, so she went to the front door and rang the bell. After a few minutes, the door was opened by her high school friend, Nora. They had an awkward moment as they paused to make sure they recognized each other, but then hugged.

"What a surprise. Come in, come in," Nora said as she stood back from the door.

Megan paused and looked behind her. Dudley was standing up in the back seat, sniffing the air outside the window and when he saw her turn around, he barked loudly. Megan turned back to Nora. "I don't know. I have the dog in the car and it's a little cold."

"Well go get him and bring him in too. This is a farm, honey, not a museum."

"Are you sure?"

"Of course, I'm sure. Go get him." Nora looked toward the dog and waved.

"That's great, thank you," Megan ran off the porch and down to the car. She opened the door a few inches and grabbed Dudley's leash. He gently jumped out of the back seat and walked with her to the front door of the farmhouse. Nora opened the door wide and welcomed them inside.

"Your house is lovely," Megan said as they stepped inside.

"It's old, but it's a great house," Nora said. She took a few minutes to show them around and when they were settled in the family room, she insisted on bringing out mugs of hot mulled cider for the ladies and water for the dog.

"I hope you like the cider," Nora said as she handed the warm mug to Megan. "It's December. We always switch to mulled cider after Thanksgiving."

Megan took a sip of her drink. "It's delicious. You'll have to give me the recipe."

"I will. My husband has family in New England. This is their secret recipe, but I'll give it to you anyway. So, Megan, how are you? I can't believe it's been years."

"I know. Thank you for reaching out when my grandmother died."

"Ah, it's nothing," Nora said. "I remember how much she meant to you. You used to talk about her all the time when we were in high school."

"She practically raised me," Megan said with a smile. "So, what about you? Tell me everything since we graduated."

Nora had a hearty, infectious laugh. "Well, the first thing is I married well. My husband, Dr. Harry Miller, works as a surgeon at

Coastal Community. We have three lovely children between the ages of five and ten. You came at a perfect time. They're in school right now, but they'll be back in thirty minutes or so. Other than our family, we do a lot with the horse farm."

"It looks beautiful," Megan said. "I didn't see a lot of it, but what I did see on the drive in was gorgeous."

"Why, thank you," Nora said with a smile. "You're going to have come back when you have time to go riding."

"Oh wow, I would absolutely love that," Megan said.

"So, what's going on, honey? I'm really glad you finally stopped in, but I also have the feeling you have something on your mind."

"Yes, I do, but I guess I must take a minute to explain things," Megan said as she reached down and scratched Dudley's head.

Nora noticed. "He's a great dog, very well behaved too."

"Yea, actually I'm fostering him right now and that's the beginning of the story I want to tell you." The two women spent the next twenty minutes talking about the Hand in Paws clinic and the animals who needed to be fostered. They talked about Dr. April May and Megan's idea about a fundraiser to be held in town square around a Christmas tree they didn't arrange for yet. When Megan was done, she took a deep breath, spread her hands and said, "Basically, that's it."

"Wow, you have been busy, but I think it's a stroke of luck you came here today."

Megan looked surprised. "Really, why?"

"Because we can help each other. If you get the permits, I think I have a perfect tree for your town square."

"That's great, but how do I help you?"

"It just so happens, the veterinarian we use for our horses is set to retire soon and I've been looking for someone. Do you think there's a chance you could get Dr. May to come out to the farm, so Harry and I could both meet her?"

"I certainly think I could," Megan said, excitement creeping into her voice. "She would love to come out and see the horses. I'm sure she would welcome any referrals you could give her as well."

"Perfect!" Nora clapped her hands together. "What if you don't get the permits?"

"I'll be very disappointed, but I'll still bring April by to meet you and Harry."

"Thank you, Megan. I'm so lucky you thought of me. It's almost like a stroke of fate."

"Stranger things have happened," Megan said with a shrug. She looked at her watch. "I'd better go. Your kids are going to be here any minute and I don't want to be in the way."

"Nonsense, they'd love to meet you and Dudley."

"And they will, one day soon. I promise," Megan said as she rose from her chair. "But I'm sure you have dinner to think about as well as homework."

Nora laughed again. "Are you sure you're not hiding any kids?"

"Believe me, that hasn't happened yet." Megan held Dudley's leash as they both made their way to the front door. Nora opened the screen to let them out and watched until they were in the car. Once settled, Megan waved as they turned in the driveway and drove away.

CHAPTER 35

egan pulled up to Misty Manor and let Dudley out of the car. He dashed to the beach and flushed a few seagulls up into the air. While she waited, Megan checked her text messages. Georgie and Amber were planning on picking up the pizza and meeting Megan at Misty Manor. Megan noted there was no text from Nick.

Megan and Dudley made their way inside the house. After a few minutes of searching, they couldn't find Marie, but Smokey was playing in the kitchen. Thinking about the pizza, Megan thought it would be a good opportunity to use the solarium. Last week, she had been going through each room, trying to clean and plan how she would like to restore them before she met the architect. Yesterday, he had called and cancelled his appointment and now with everything else going on, Megan thought it might be better to wait until Spring to discuss renovations anyway.

The solarium was a beautiful room on the Northeast corner of the house. Originally, it may have been part of the open porch but sometime in the last 100 years, large glass windows had enclosed the area which sat on the corner of the wraparound porch.

The room was very comfortable and afforded gorgeous views of the Point with the lighthouse as well as the ocean. Megan had started cleaning the windows and vacuuming the furniture last week while wondering why they hadn't bothered to grace the room in the last six months she was there. During summer, nothing was nicer than the rocking chairs and porch swing on the outdoor porch, but in the winter, the solarium would be one of the nicest rooms in the house. The only other similar area would be the cupola, but Megan wanted to save the attic and cupola as a private spot for herself.

After an hour or so, the doorbell rang. Georgie and Amber popped into the foyer with two pizzas, IPA beer and a cold bottle of wine. "Wow, who's going to eat all this pizza?"

"Georgie insisted on meatball and I didn't want meat, so we ordered a thin crust, well done cheese pizza as well," Amber said with a pout. "I still have to count every carb that goes in my mouth and I prefer a nice light wine instead of beer."

Georgie rolled her eyes and Megan laughed. Last night she had the most elegant of meals, tonight was a variety of pizza and drinks. She wished it was mid-summer again and they were eating on the beach in the warm weather.

The girls were headed toward the kitchen when Megan stopped them. "No wait, let's go into the solarium to eat."

"Where?" Georgie asked, confused as they always ran to the kitchen.

"Tonight, we're going to the solarium, right through the living room," Megan said as she pointed.

The three girls walked toward the room and stepped over the threshold.

"I remember being in here when we were in high school," Georgie said as she approached a table. "Can I put the food down here?"

"Sure, of course."

"What a great room," Amber said as she looked around. "That fireplace is gorgeous. Look at that stonework."

"I've been cleaning it out," Megan explained. "When I first came in here, there were sheets over the furniture and things piled in the corner. I have a feeling it hasn't been used since before Hurricane

Sandy. Afterwards, Grandma Rose moved back to Misty Manor but probably wasn't well enough to do a lot with the house. I'm sure someone went through each room to make sure there weren't broken windows and such, but then the rooms have remained untouched. I keep telling myself to ask Billy, he probably knows about that."

"You know, I remember seeing all the windows in the lower part of Misty Manor boarded up before the storm," Amber said. "I should ask Tommy if he knows anything."

"It appears someone was here before and after the storm, that's for sure," Georgie said. "We'd be happy to help you clean out whatever you want. You're going to need a lot of help at some point."

"Yes, I can see that," Megan said as she walked over and started a fire. She had laid all the wood in anticipation of their dinner. Dudley and Smokey immediately walked over and made themselves comfortable by the fire.

"Do you think you'll eventually turn Misty Manor into a bed and breakfast?" Amber asked as she started pouring a glass of wine. She held the bottle poised over a second glass. "Megan, are you having wine or beer?"

"I think I'll have the wine," Megan said looking back and forth between the two. "I had some delicious wine last night."

"And that brings us to the reason for our get-together," Georgie said. "We want to hear all the details about dinner."

"I'll tell you about it, but I don't think it's going to be as exciting as you think."

"You never know," Amber said, plucking a slice of cheese pizza out of the box. "We bought the food, so spill."

"We watched out the window until you two drove off in the Jag," Georgie said as she took a swig of beer.

"Yes, that Jag is a very nice car and Jonathan is very sweet, polite and handsome."

"We saw that," Amber said. "What else?"

"Wow, you want every detail? You two are ruthless."

"Start talking." Georgie made a "hurry up" gesture with her hand as she chewed.

"Okay, so we went to the Portside and it's very fancy. Not anything I could afford on a regular basis. You're greeted by hostesses, a maître d', sommeliers, and a lot of supporting staff."

Georgie turned to Amber. "What's a sommelier?"

"You know, like a wine expert. They tell you what the right wine for your food would be."

"Oh, maybe I could do that for beer. We have a lot of good IPA's in New Jersey now."

Amber elbowed her while making a frown. "Oh, hush up." Turning to Megan she said. "Go ahead, what happened next?"

Megan told them about their meal and how nice it was for Teddy and Jonathan to see each other again. She also told them about the plans they made for the town tree lighting and fundraiser. "I'm just waiting to hear from Ellen if she made any progress with town hall today."

"Uh, oh," Georgie said as she licked her fingers of all the pizza sauce. "Does she have to go through your buddy, Mayor Davenport? If so, you're going to have a problem."

"That's why it's better that Ellen does it instead of me," Megan said. "Can you imagine me having to meet with that guy again?"

"No, not really," Georgie said. "Let her and Teddy handle it."

"Yes, I agree, they can do the official stuff, but we have to discuss setting up the fundraiser, the tree, and organizing the walk."

"Where are we going to get a tree big enough for town square?" Amber asked as she sipped her wine.

"That's the surprise I have for you two," Megan said as she jumped up. "When Grandma Rose died, I got a card from one of our high-school friends. They live on a horse farm and raise Christmas trees, so I went to see her this afternoon."

"Who?" Amber demanded immediately.

"You ready?" Megan teased.

"Enough already, who is it?"

"Nora, remember her? She's now Nora Miller and she lives near Colt's Neck."

"Nora? Get out," Georgie said. "She was always so quiet in school. I thought she moved out of state."

"Turns out she didn't and she's in a magnificent house on a large horse farm."

"Very nice. I would love to see it one day," Amber said. "Do you think she has a big enough tree?"

"She didn't show it to me, but she said they have one on the farm," Megan said. "I haven't told anyone else yet, because if it doesn't work out, I don't want to get everyone excited."

"That's fantastic," Amber said. "We could pull this off, yet."

"When will you find out about the permits?"

"Hopefully, the minute they're approved," Megan said.

The ladies continued to chat as they ate and drank. "I'm noticing there's one person I haven't heard you talk about tonight," Georgie said as she finished her pizza and left the table. She walked toward the windows and sat on one of the couches with a beautiful ocean view. The sky was dark as usual in December, but there was a relaxing view of lights in the distance over the water. To the side, they could see the lighthouse with the revolving lamp in the lantern room.

"Yea, him," Megan said with a frown as she scratched Dudley's head.

"Uh, oh," Amber said. "What's going on there?"

"I don't know. I went to the clinic this morning because it was the first day for Dr. April May and I wanted to wish her well."

"That name still cracks me up," Georgie said, as he shook her head.

"Yes, I told her I'll just call her April from now on," Megan said. "Anyway, Nick showed up and he was a bit testy. He must have had friends working security at the Portside because he knew all about the dinner."

"Uh, oh," Amber said, eyebrows raised. "Trouble in paradise, already."

"I honestly don't know why. Nothing happened, and he won't tell me anything about the investigation which is making me mad."

"He's not allowed to tell you anything, right?" Amber said, defending him.

"Technically, yes," Megan said as she moved over to the couches as well. "But I have a feeling he's trying to keep me out of it to protect me more than anything."

"And what's wrong with that?" Georgie asked. "You've gotten yourself in a few scrapes since you came back to New Jersey."

Megan turned toward her friend. "Who's counting?"

Georgie held her hands up in self-defense. "Just saying, it may be for your benefit. He may be protecting you as you say, or he may not be allowed to share."

"I know women who could do worse," Amber chimed in.

"Well, he wasn't very nice today for someone I'm supposedly seeing, if that's what we officially are, and I haven't heard a word from him since."

"I wonder who told him about your date with Jonathan?" Amber asked, eyes wide open.

"It wasn't a date," Megan said, shaking her head.

"Well maybe it wasn't labeled as such, but between the roses and everything else, it had some energy going on there, if you know what I mean."

"The last thing I need to get involved with is energy, from either one of them." Megan stood up and threw her paper plate on the table. She combined the remaining pieces of pizza into one box and collected the garbage into the other. "Anyway, Nick hasn't called or texted, so I don't think he even cares."

Georgie rolled her eyes at Amber and started humming. "Well, dinner was great. I enjoyed that very much."

"Me too," Amber said as she poured another two ounces of wine in her glass. "Anyway, back to the fundraiser. Let's assume the permits go through. We need to make of list of everything we need to do."

While Amber and Georgie exchanged raised eyebrows over their drinks, Megan left to collect some pens and paper from her grandmother's small office off the foyer and pouted the entire way.

CHAPTER 36

*M*icky got out of his car and slammed the door. He studied the front door and specifically the locks of the Hand in Paws Animal Clinic. Pulling the door open, he heard a bell jingle as he stepped into the front room. Immediately, a volunteer in a green smock, embroidered with dog paws, greeted him. "Welcome to Hand in Paws. My name is Judy. Can I help you?"

"Oh," Micky said as he jumped at her voice. He then wiped at his nose as he felt the first drip down his face. His allergy to dogs made it difficult to case out these clinics. Within minutes, he'd be sneezing and blowing his nose. "I'm actually looking for doggie biscuits. I'd like to bring some home to my dog."

"Oh, how sweet," Judy said. "What type of dog do you have?"

"Ah, I think it's a Westie, but I'm not sure," Micky shrugged. "I don't know. It's my wife's dog." He rubbed at his nose as the itching increased. Across the room, his eyes connected with Jared. He had to make sure there was no connection between the two. Jared had his scarf on, despite the fact the clinic was well heated today. Micky noted Jared was perspiring.

"Well, we have wonderful doggie cookies and the perfect size for a Westie."

"Oh, thank you. Could you show me where they are?" Micky followed the woman through various aisles. She made a very circuitous route around the clinic and somehow managed to walk him through both rooms. They walked past the surgical arena and Micky made note of the door to the supply closet. Micky was very appreciative of the tour and noted where the cameras were, the cages, as well as the high-end merchandise. Jared had tried to describe the clinic's back room as well as the back door, but Micky had to check the place himself. He didn't trust Jared's description of the rooms or security. They only had to make one more score before they could stop working in this clinic. Micky already had the next target picked, but he knew Hand in Paws had a large narcotic shipment on the way as well as two pedigreed dogs to be adopted as Christmas presents within the next week. Once they were paid for the take, he could afford to stop for a couple of weeks and then move on to the next county.

"Here we are," Judy said. "These are the best doggie cookies we have, and they would make a wonderful Christmas gift for that special dog in your life."

Micky shook his head. "They look very nice."

"You buy them by the pound so if you tell me how many pounds you want, I'll be sure to wrap them up for you real nice."

"Oh, how about two pounds then?"

"Of course, don't forget we have some beautiful ornaments with pictures of Westies on them. You could pick one up for your holiday tree," the woman suggested.

"Thank you but I think the cookies will be enough," Micky said as he nodded. As she weighed, measured and bagged the cookies, Micky looked around the room. Once again, he noted the room, the doors, and the security in the area. Jared told him the dogs were coming Saturday afternoon. They were supposed to stay at the clinic for a day or two to be immunized, chipped and registered, but Micky didn't want to delay the heist because he knew the adoptive family would be excited and want to see them as soon as possible. Jared also told him the narcotics were coming today, so Saturday was the day.

Micky followed the woman to a counter where she rang up his purchase. He paid for the cookies after sneezing in his hand and wiping it off on his pants. Judy was reluctant to take the money but held it by the corner and placed it in the back of the cash box. Micky took his dog cookies and left the clinic.

CHAPTER 37

Megan was standing on the beach, her hands pushed into her jacket. She had walked her friends to their car and needed to let Dudley roam around to do his business. While she waited she gazed at the stars and the beautiful December night. The air was warmer than expected and the pounding of the waves on the beach was soothing. All in all, it was a beautiful night at the shore.

Dudley ran up and nudged her hand. She gave him a quick pet. "Are you ready to go inside? We need to check on Smokey."

As they walked up to the porch, Dudley paused and the hair on his back stood up. Megan stopped behind him when she realized something was wrong. He neither barked nor growled but stood guard with Megan beside him.

"Megan," a voice said from the dark.

Megan jumped, and Dudley looked over to the side. He paused a moment, then began wagging his tail. Megan noticed his form relaxing before she saw Nick step out of the shadows.

"Nick, you scared me. What are you doing hiding in the dark?"

"I wasn't hiding. I just arrived a short time ago and I saw you had company. I didn't want to butt in, but then you all came outside, and I thought it would be better to wait until your friends left."

"What's wrong with you? You've been acting so strange," Megan asked as she looked at him.

Nick looked down as he clenched his jaw. "Nothing. This investigation has been aggravating."

"You won't talk to me and this morning you were positively rude," Megan said. "What did I do to you?"

"Nothing," Nick admitted.

"So, then what's up?" Megan asked again. When Nick paused, she tried again. "Nick, either talk to me or go home. Standing here brooding is not helping anything."

"Okay, okay," Nick said, raising his hands. "But you have to swear to keep all this to yourself. Do not tell anyone or I could be fired, and we could lose the perp."

"Okay, I promise already," Megan said. "Come in to the solarium. The fire is still burning, and I need you to tell me everything."

They walked into the solarium and Nick walked over to the fire. "I've never been in this room. You have a gorgeous view of the ocean." Looking through the windows, they saw the lighthouse, a fishing boat gliding along the ocean and lights in the distance.

"The view in the daytime is beautiful as well," Megan said. "You can see the ocean, all the way up around the point and the lighthouse. It's a great room when you need to be inside."

Megan led Nick to the couch. Dudley followed and curled up on the floor by their feet. "You should put a Christmas tree in here," Nick said.

"That's a great idea. I was up in the attic and saw some of the beautiful ornaments Rose kept."

"Let me know when. I'll be happy to help out."

"I was going to ask you to help me decorate the porch and windows. I didn't see any outdoor decorations in the attic, so I'll have to go buy some things."

"I'll go with you," Nick said glumly.

"Thanks, I really appreciate that. So now what's going on with the animal clinic? I went there today to welcome April and let her know

I'm available if she has any questions. You were kind of tense today and I don't know why."

Nick took a deep breath and blew out the air. He put his hands up and pushed back his hair. "There's a lot of pressure with this investigation because they think it's a gang or something. Several clinics in the area have been hit in the last several months and they think it's the same group, but no one has been able to get an angle on them."

"There's nothing that ties them together?"

"The only thing I can come up with is the volunteers. There are four volunteers that have worked at several of the clinics that have been hit. None of them have previous criminal records and it all may be coincidental because volunteers do work in various places, but that's all I've got."

"Do you honestly think they would try again with all the attention the clinic is getting now?"

"It's very possible. Teddy confirmed for me that another large order for opioids was placed and delivered today. As you know, the safe had been cleaned out again. With the new shipment, we'll wait and watch, but surveillance or not, sometimes the perps are just that good. We'll catch them eventually, that's for sure."

"Is April safe working in the clinic?" Megan was concerned for the new veterinarian.

"She'll have Carlos working with her. That should help."

"Who'll help Carlos if someone pulls a gun? Just because there are two people doesn't mean they're safe."

Nick paused for a moment and seemed to be debating with himself.

Megan pushed his shoulder. "What? What aren't you telling me?"

"Carlos is undercover. He's a cop. He'll be more than able to defend them and take out the perp if it comes to that."

"Really?" Megan asked surprised. "Does April know that?"

"No, and don't tell her," Nick said. "I'm serious. People act differently when they have knowledge of certain things. Their reactions are different in a critical situation. It's better if she doesn't know, so don't tell her. Promise me," Nick said as he looked directly into her eyes.

"Okay, I promise," Megan said. "Cross my heart."

"Thank you."

"That still doesn't explain why you were in such a bad mood this morning."

Nick frowned and looked out the window. After a moment he said, "I'm still upset about your dinner last night."

"So what?" Megan asked sharply. "What about it?"

"Well, it's just very interesting this guy shows up right after you inherit the house and some money."

"He's Teddy's son," Megan protested. "My grandmother was involved in a lot of things and I have no clue how to do what she did, so he's helping me out."

"Why isn't Teddy helping you?"

"I don't know, exactly." Megan shrugged. "I got the impression Teddy was thinking of retiring. Working with Jonathan would be like working with one of his younger partners."

"It would be mighty convenient if he suddenly decided to propose to keep Misty Manor and Rose's estate in the family, wouldn't it?"

"I don't believe this," Megan said as she stood up. "Green does not look good on you, Nick. I've given you no reason to be jealous and hell, I don't even know where our relationship stands to be honest with you."

"What if I'm just trying to protect you?" Nick protested as he stood as well. "Do you know how many people have accused me of being a gold-digger? I have no idea what you're actually worth now, but don't forget I was here before you inherited anything."

"So, let me get this straight. Because you're suspicious of Jonathan, you decided to be a jerk to me this morning? That's makes no sense at all."

Nick shifted and looked down for a moment. He took a deep breath and looked back up at her. "You're completely right and yes I was jealous. One of my buddies was working security there last night and called me about your dinner party."

"Oh great, so you did have someone spying on me?"

"I don't have anyone spying on you, he just told me what he saw."

"Then stop listening and stop assuming what's going on," Megan said with tears in her eyes as she walked over to the windows. Hurt, she stood with her arms wrapped around her stomach as she swallowed.

The room was silent for a moment before Nick came up behind her and placed his hands on her shoulders. He whispered into the back of ear. "Look, I'm sorry. It's just that after all these years, I've finally found you again and I swear I'd throw myself off one of the jetties if something happened to you. I worry about you in general and now I'm going to have to fight off all these guys trying to take advantage of your new social status."

Megan shook her head as tears slid down her cheeks. She turned to face him. "I guess just being honest and talking to me isn't enough?"

Nick looked into her eyes. He lifted his right hand, tucked her hair behind her ear and whispered. "I'm sorry. I haven't really said it, but I'm very much in love with you and I want you to be in love with me. I know the past six months have been hell for you, so I haven't pushed on our relationship but now I'm kicking myself for that because I've left room for other guys to move in."

Megan took her hand and placed it over Nicks on her cheek. She turned toward his hand and lightly kissed his palm. He quickly pulled her close and his lips were suddenly crushing hers. He kissed her neck while holding her close and whispered into her hair. "I love you so much." Their kiss was then slower, deeper as they felt the anger dissolve between them. Megan placed her head on Nick's shoulder while he hugged her tightly. They stood there for a moment, not saying anything, unsure of what to do next, when suddenly Nick's cell phone started ringing. He cursed softly. "I'll ignore it." They kissed again, more lightly when the phone started chiming again.

Megan pulled back. "You better answer it, Nick. It could be important."

Angry, he pulled the cell phone out of his pocket and walked toward the opposite side of the room. "Yeah?" Nick yelled into the phone. He listened as someone on the other end rattled off some information of which Megan could understand none. "I'll be there in ten."

Nick turned toward Megan. She smiled, aware the mood had been broken regardless of the outcome. "Just go, it's okay."

He approached her and held her lightly around the waist. "Can I call you later?"

"Let's not make any promises. Who knows how long you'll be tied up. Just go do what you have to, and we'll take it step by step."

Cursing softly, Nick leaned down and kissed Megan once more on the lips. He whispered, "I'll call you as soon as I can."

She nodded and said, "I'll be waiting. Let me walk you to the door."

CHAPTER 38

*M*egan awoke the next morning with Dudley and Smokey beside her. She had waited up a while but then went to bed. Leaning over to the side table, she checked her phone. Nick hadn't called. She stretched and rolled over, pushed the animals off the bed and got ready for the day. As she was walking downstairs, her cell phone began to chirp.

"Hello?"

"Megan? Good morning, it's Ellen."

"Oh hi, how are you?"

"Very well, thank you. Teddy asked me to give you a call."

"Did we have any luck yesterday at town hall?"

"To be honest, they weren't overly eager to help us," Ellen said. "We pointed out the tradition is meant for the whole town to participate and spread some holiday spirit."

"Uh oh," Megan said. "Did Mayor Davenport throw up a road block for us?"

"Perhaps a bit, but Teddy went in and spoke to them and they finally relented."

"What did they want?" Megan asked as she poured herself a mug of coffee.

"He had to promise we would make all the arrangements. We must get the tree and pay for security and insurance for the event and Teddy agreed. He felt that was more than fair."

"So, we got the permits?" Megan asked excitedly.

"I got a call this morning," Ellen said. "The permits are ready. If we can find a tree, we can make plans."

"That's fantastic," Megan said. "As a matter of fact, I have a friend who owns a horse farm. She told me she would donate a tree as soon as we secured the permits. Should I call her and share the good news, or should we wait?"

"Why don't you wait until I have them in the palm of my hand, just in case," Ellen suggested. "I'll text you as soon as I pick them up."

"Great, thank you, Ellen. I have a little something I need to do first anyway."

"Excellent. I'll let you go then. We'll touch base later today. I think this will be a special event for the town. It'll bring some of the spirit back where it belongs. Thank you, Megan."

"Thank you and I can't wait to hear from you," Megan said before she hung up the phone. She turned around to find the pets staring at her in the kitchen. Megan fed them and let them take care of business.

When they were done, she grabbed her keys and turned around to call Dudley. He was already by the car with his leash in his mouth. Megan laughed as she closed the front door and headed for the car.

They drove to the animal clinic and parked near the curb. Dudley popped out of the car as soon as Megan opened the door. He held his own leash in his mouth as they made their way up to the back door.

Megan gave a slight knock and opened the door into the back of the clinic. No one was there when she stepped into the room. Dudley followed her inside and she closed the door to keep out the cold. After several moments, Megan made her way toward the front of the clinic. Looking through the door, she saw April and Carlos helping a customer with a sick dog. Around the aisles, the volunteers were feeding, cleaning and playing with the animals.

April finally looked up and saw Megan standing in the doorway between the two rooms. She waved and walked over. "Hi, how are you today?"

"Fine, I don't want to disturb you, but I wanted to talk to you about something," Megan said. "Do you have a minute?"

April turned around to see how Carlos was making out with the dog. When it appeared that he had things under control, she drew Megan into the back room.

"Sorry, it can get a bit crazy around here," April said.

"How are you making out?" Megan said. "Are you getting used to the clinic?"

"Yes, I'm coming along," April said as she looked around the room. "I learn new things every day and I'll eventually get used to the process around here."

"Have you had any trouble?"

"Nothing except sick animals."

"I'm glad to hear that," Megan said. "Although, I thought I would find you in the back, so I walked right through the back door. Considering everything that happened, maybe that door should be locked, from the inside, at least."

"You're right. I didn't realize it was open. Maybe Teddy can send someone to look at it for me."

"I'm sure he can," Megan said with a smile. "I'll call him for you."

"Thanks, I'd appreciate that. What else can I help you with? I'm guessing you had something more on your mind."

"I do, and it involves both of us," Megan said excitedly.

April looked surprised. "How so?"

"I had this idea of having a fundraiser for the clinic," Megan said.

"I remember you saying so, the night I was interviewed."

"Yes, I wanted to restart some of our traditions in town. We have an Ocean Holiday Walk down the boardwalk. People decorate their homes and boats in the marina. If it's a nice night, it's a beautiful walk. It ends in town square where we light the tree. Every family brings a decoration to put on the tree and we have tables set up with cookies and hot chocolate. We also have tables as part of the Holly Berry Craft fair where you can buy ornaments, decorations and other crafts. We have a local band who has volunteered to play music. The nicest thing is part of the proceeds will go to the Hand in Paws Animal Clinic."

"That sounds wonderful," April said. "How can I help?"

"Well, I think it will help you too, but let me explain. I have a friend who owns a large horse farm near Colts Neck. She also grows trees and offered to donate one to the town square for the event."

"In exchange for what?" April asked through squinted eyes.

Megan laughed. "You saw right through me. The veterinarian she uses is retiring and she asked me to find her a new one. I immediately thought of you. So, it's a win-win situation. You said you wanted to start visiting some of the local horse farms and I have someone in need of your services. Will you go meet the owners?"

April smiled and shook Megan's hand. "Consider it done."

"Great, everything is coming together," Megan said.

"So far, so good," April said. "I think whoever targeted this place has gone elsewhere."

"I hope so," Megan said. "You just never know what's going to happen next."

CHAPTER 39

"So how did it go?" Jared asked as he rubbed the back of his neck.

"It went okay," Micky said. "I saw everything I needed to see. I'm not happy I have to help out with this."

"I'm still sick," Jared said. "I'm tired and nauseous. My neck is full of pus."

"And probably going straight to your brain. You're lucky they haven't figured you out. For cryin' out loud, you were wearing that scarf and sweating like a pig in there today. I told you to get some antibiotics and straighten yourself out."

"Where the hell was I going to get them? You said I couldn't go to the hospital. I'm sure the police put out a BOLO for someone with a stab wound and I didn't find an opportunity to steal any antibiotics worth the effort."

"You're a stupid ass for getting stabbed in the first place."

Jared threw an empty beer can at Micky. "Hey, if you're getting some of the profits, you're gonna do some of the work. I can't carry two dogs and a stash of narcotics anyway. Two guys, in and out, the boss is happy, and we're done. I'm tired of this crap."

"Don't let the boss hear you say that," Micky said as he let out a loud burp.

"Half of me doesn't care anymore," Jared said as rubbed his jaw. "I just want to get this over with."

CHAPTER 40

"What do you think of this one?" Megan asked Nick as she picked up a five-foot candy cane covered with bright LED lights. "This would look nice. We could get a couple of them and line the walkway."

"I like it," Nick said. The two had met at the local mart to purchase decorations for the porch and windows of Misty Manor. Nick pushed a cart loaded with lights, garlands, ribbons and large bows for the rails and posts on the porch. The traditional lights and decorations would look great on the Grand Victorian home, but Megan wanted to get something special. The front door would hold a nice big wreath decorated with pine cones, sprigs of white twigs with berries, gold and red Christmas ornaments and a lovely bow. They agreed to the candy canes for the walkway and large brightly lit stars around the widow's walk on the top of the house. In between, they decided on green and red lights surrounding the front and sides of the house.

"I can't wait," Megan said excitedly. "The house is going to look great this year." She smiled brightly, leaned up on her toes and gave Nick a kiss on the cheek. "Thank you so much for doing this with me."

He hugged her around the waist. "This is going to take a few hours. You'd better order some tasty food and drink."

"You got it," Megan said as they pushed the cart up to the checkout counter. "The town started decorating the boardwalk today. They put wreaths on the benches and hung angels on the light posts along the way. I can't wait to see it lit up at night." They handed the decorations to the clerk, so she could scan them at the register. The purchase was costly, but Megan handed over the new credit card she had been given by Teddy. She knew it had a high limit and the two hundred million she had inherited was hers to spend as she pleased. She insisted that none of her friends knew how much she was worth and she planned to keep it that way. They pushed the cart toward the car and Megan was glad they had used her old SUV because the decorations wouldn't have fit in Nick's Camaro. Finally loaded, they drove to Misty Manor to decorate.

Megan ordered food and the couple spent the next several hours decorating the porch. After what felt like miles of electric cords, they had finished everything except the stars for the widow's walk. "We'll have to go through the attic and up to the roof to hang the stars. Are you ready for that?"

"Ready when you are," Nick said as he grabbed the pile of stars. He handed lights and electric cords to Megan. "Let's go."

The couple walked into Misty Manor and up two flights of the grand staircase. Arriving on the third floor, they walked down the hall and then up the final flight to the attic. Megan pulled out the key and then turned to Nick.

"I'm going to show you the cupola. It was one of my favorite places to hide when I was a kid, and it's beautiful. I'll show you the attic, too. No one goes in the attic except me because Rose put her valuables up here before the storm."

"Can't wait," Nick said with a smile.

Megan continued talking as she unlocked the door. "Once we're in the attic, we have to climb one more flight up to the widow's walk. Depending on the breeze, we have to be careful up there."

"Believe me, I'm not in the mood to fall off the roof of this house."

"Not unless you can fly."

"Do you have electric in the attic?" Nick shifted the stars to his other hand. They were several feet high and difficult to carry.

"There's some but I'm not sure how much or even how old the wiring is. I didn't think of that beforehand," Megan said.

"Okay, I'll look once we get up there."

Megan unlocked the door and they both walked into the attic. "Put the decorations down for a moment."

Megan toured Nick around the attic. They moved a few boxes to look for outlets and electrical access. Then Megan showed Nick the cupola and let him know her plans of painting and refreshing the furniture. They went to the windows and couldn't see the water as it was turning dark but saw the lighthouse as well as a lit bridge in the distance.

Leaving the room, they walked up the lone flight of stairs to the roof, opened the door and stepped out onto the widow's walk. Megan grabbed Nick's hand as they made their way toward the front of the house. The wind was cold, but they were able to hear the rush of the water and look down at the beach. Dudley had followed them into the attic but was unable to climb the last flight to the roof. He watched from down below and barked.

"This is really something," Nick said looking around. "It's really high up here."

"Yes," Megan said as the wind blew her hair off her face. "You should see it during the day. You can see the ocean for miles and the beach is gorgeous. The only better view is from the lighthouse. I'll have to take you up there sometime."

"At least that'll be indoors. You can't miss a step up here."

"Please be careful. We can just forget it if there's no electric or you don't want to put the stars up here."

"I didn't say that, yet," Nick said, looking around.

"Okay, tell me what we need to do next," Megan said.

"Just this." Nick wrapped his arms around her waist and kissed her on the lips. When they pulled back he smiled and leaned his forehead against hers. "You can get a real rush from that up here."

"Yes, but it would be safer in the cupola so let's go downstairs and decide what we have to do."

"You got it." Nick held onto Megan as they made their way back toward the door which led down to the attic. "Okay, let me look around for a few minutes and get to work. I think it would be best to just let me handle things up here."

Megan looked at him for a moment and nodded. "Just be safe, please."

"I will, maybe there are a few boxes you can deal with up here somewhere."

"Yes, I'm sure there's work I can do." They spent the next hour working quietly together. Nick connected the electric and ran it up to the widow's walk and then one by one, brought the stars outside and wired them to the small fence surrounding the area and plugged them in.

In the meantime, Megan continued to work through the pile of Christmas decorations in the corner. She made a smaller pile of her favorite ornaments and brought them to the spare bedroom downstairs. Next, she unwrapped some of her favorite room decorations. A Christmas dollhouse, Christmas mermaid, ceramic carousel, Santa with a surfboard, indoor garlands, wreaths and candles. She found a wooden advent calendar house and a box of Santas representing many countries around the world.

Megan brought them all downstairs and began to sort them on the bed. She dipped into the ornament box and took out each one. She came upon a box of photos that had been made into ornaments and was fascinated as she looked through them. Over the next hour, she studied photos of her great-grandparents, grandparents, and parents. There were photos of her as a young girl and looking at them brought back memories of them hanging on the tree, but she didn't remember the photos of the rest of the family. There was a photo of her being held by her mom as a baby. She was wearing a beautiful hand sewn Christmas dress.

Tears began to slide down her cheeks as memories from when she was a young child began to float back to her. She wiped her eyes with her sleeve and looked through the rest of the box. At the bottom, she found a photo ornament of her grandmother holding a dog who was busy licking her face. Grandmother Rose was laughing and appeared very happy in the photo. Megan could tell the photo had been taken years before she was born and made her wonder what happened to the dog and why Rose had never adopted another.

"Hey, come up here," Nick yelled from the attic. "I want you to see something."

"Coming," Megan said as she placed the ornament on the bed. She ran up into the attic where Nick took her hand and guided her back up to the roof.

"I'd tell you to close your eyes, but I'm too worried you'd fall off."

Megan laughed and followed Nick into the night. He led her to the middle of the widow's walk. "Well, what do you think?"

Megan slowly turned and looked around. "It's beautiful," she said as she beamed. "Nick, you did a fantastic job. It's absolutely beautiful."

"I have something else to show you." He took her back into the attic and led her to the cupola. Each window in the cupola was also lit up with a star.

"What a great idea," Megan said as she looked at the windows. "Let's go outside and see how it looks from the beach."

"Okay, first let me wrap up the rest of the electric cords and we'll go."

The two of them ran down the grand staircase, grabbed an extra coat and with Dudley running along beside them, made their way to the beach. Megan didn't stop until they reached the water and after a moment she slowly turned around. "Here goes," she said. Her first look made her gasp and she found herself crying again. The entire house was illuminated with colorful lights and decorations. "Wow, I wish Rose could be here right now. She would absolutely love it. It's breathtaking. The last few Christmas's here must have been so depressing with the house dark."

Nick held her around the waist. "Megan, I'm sure your grandmother and all of heaven can see the house now and are smiling down on us."

Megan held his hands with hers. "I hope so, Nick. I really hope so."

CHAPTER 41

*M*egan arrived in town square the next day. She had received a phone call early in the morning the tree was being delivered around noon and she wanted to be there to receive it. She parked her car and climbed out. While waiting she looked up at the decorations on the light posts and those strung across the street. She hadn't felt this excited in a long time.

Within a half hour an oversized truck showed up with a twenty-five-foot Douglas Fir tied to it. Megan and Dudley watched as men from town helped to set up the tree and secure it in the custom-made base. They agreed to wrap lights around the tree to be lit during the event next weekend. In the meantime, the town residents and guests were welcomed to start placing ornaments of their choice.

"Looks lovely, doesn't it?"

Megan jumped at the voice at her side. "Jonathan, what a surprise. What are you doing here?"

"I was at the bookstore and when I walked out, I wanted to see what all the excitement was about. I walked over and here you were."

"Ah, I see," Megan said. "Well to answer your question, it does look lovely. I don't think they've had a tree in the town square for several years so this is very exciting."

"It sure is and it's all due to you," Jonathan said. He looked hand-some in a grey wool suit with matching vest.

"Well, I may have thought of it, but thanks to you and Teddy and Ellen, this is finally happening."

"It benefits everyone and will bring morale and business to the town, so they could hardly say no," Jonathan said, his English accent apparent.

"Thanks, Jonathan."

"It's nice to see you smiling," Jonathan said. "It takes some of the radiance away from the tree."

Megan flushed as Jonathan looked at her.

"I had a wonderful time at dinner the other night," Jonathan said as he smiled. "I'm looking forward to the Christmas party tomorrow."

"Me too," Megan said as Dudley pulled on his leash. Megan quickly looked down and saw a boy had come over to pet Dudley and had just finished feeding him a luscious chocolate brownie. "Oh no, don't do that. I don't think dogs are supposed to have chocolate."

The boy suddenly looked scared. He didn't say anything, but sensing he did something wrong he ran away before he got in trouble.

"Will he be okay?" Jonathan asked as he looked at the dog.

"He looks okay," Megan said. "Maybe, I'll call April to be sure."

"I think that would be well advised," Jonathan said.

"Okay, let me go then," Megan said. "I'll see you at the Christmas party."

Jonathan took her hand and kissed it gently. "Looking forward to it."

Megan blushed as she tugged on Dudley's leash and walked away.

CHAPTER 42

"*A*re you feeling okay?" Megan asked Dudley as he lay on the back seat with his head on top of his paws. "You seem quiet." When Dudley didn't stand up or look out the window, Megan began to worry. "I guess it's right back to the Hand in Paws Animal Clinic for you."

Megan concentrated on the road until her cell starting ringing. She reached out and pushed the green button. "Hello?"

"Hi Megan, it's Georgie."

"Hi, how are you?"

"Pretty well. I wanted to reach out and see what's been happening. The Christmas party is tomorrow. I tried calling last night but you didn't answer."

Megan paused for a moment. "That's because I was decorating Misty Manor with Nick."

"Really? So, you two are talking again?"

"Yes, he showed up after you two left the other night and we had a long chat. I think we smoothed things over."

"Did he ask about Jonathan?"

"Well he had some comments about him. He's a very nice, handsome man. But our relationship is strictly business."

"Are you sure about that?"

"Why would someone like Jonathan be interested in someone like me?"

"Okay, let's not go there. Not enough time in the world for that conversation."

"Hey, let me ask you something. I happen to have been with Jonathan a few minutes ago in the town square. We were watching them put up the Christmas tree that Nora sent over."

"That's an interesting thing to do with a business contact," Georgie said sarcastically.

"Anyway, we were talking, and I was a bit distracted."

"You think? Yea, just business. I got it."

"Georgie, just shut up and listen. Anyway, I looked down at Dudley and some kid had given him this gooey, luscious, very rich, fudge brownie. Dudley had eaten the whole thing."

"Oh, that's bad," Georgie said. "Is he okay?"

Megan's stomach knotted. "He's lying on the back seat with his head on his paws. Normally he's sitting up."

"You know dogs can't have chocolate," Georgie said. "You'd better bring him to April right away."

"I'm already on my way over there," Megan said. "I hope he's okay."

"Well, just let her check him and tell you what to do," Georgie said.

"I should be there in ten minutes," Megan said.

"Let me know what she says. In the meantime, I wanted to ask about tomorrow. What's the plan?"

"Why don't you come over to my place and then we can all go together?"

"Sounds good to me," Georgie said. "Did you finish all the decorating?

"Yes," Megan said. "Nick and I went to the store last night, bought all new outdoor decorations and spent the night putting everything up. It looks great in the dark, so you can see it tonight."

"Can't wait," Georgie said. "Ever since we advertised the Christmas Holiday Walk, everyone is decorating. It's almost like old times."

"I love it when everything is decorated. It's so pretty," Megan said as she pulled up to the curb. "I'm at the animal clinic so let me go."

"Alright, I hope Dudley is okay. Let me know what happens."

"Will do, gotta go."

Several minutes later, Megan was walking through the front door of the Hand in Paws Animal Clinic.

The first person she met was Judy Bowan. "Hello, Dearie. How are you?" When Judy saw Megan's face she said, "Is everything alright?"

Megan explained her situation with Dudley and asked to see April right away.

"Oh, of course. Let me find her."

Within minutes, April came to the front of the clinic to greet Megan and Dudley. "Hi," she said as she leaned down and petted Dudley on the head. "Why don't we go in the back and you can tell me what happened."

The trio moved to an exam room and April helped Dudley on to the table. He had no symptoms except being sluggish.

"Is he going to be okay?" Megan asked.

"He looks alright, so far," April said as he continued to examine him.

"What kind of symptoms does chocolate cause in dogs?'

"Well, symptoms can last up to 72 hours, but the first twelve hours are the most dangerous, if they've eaten enough chocolate to poison them."

"What should I look for?"

"Always watch out for vomiting, diarrhea, muscle spasms, or agitation or nervousness. Sometimes dogs get very agitated, and pace, or pant. In bad cases, a dog can have seizures."

Megan's face looked stricken. "What should I do?"

"Just take him home and keep an eye on him. If anything changes you can bring him right back." April flashed a confident yet compassionate smile.

"You'll be here this weekend?"

"Yes, I will," April said in a whisper. "Between you and me, we are receiving two dogs tomorrow that will be adopted at Christmas.

They're a rare breed so I must tag them and keep them safe this weekend. The owner will be coming on Sunday to adopt."

"Have you had any sign of trouble?" Megan asked as she looked behind her.

"Nothing," April said with a smile. "But we did receive our narcotic shipment, so I've been keeping a very close eye on that, too."

Megan didn't want to say too much but asked, "Are things going okay with Carlos here?"

"Yes, fine. He's a nice guy."

"Good, I'm glad to hear that," Megan said as she gave Dudley a pat. She stood up and looked at April. "Are you going to the Christmas party tomorrow?"

"No, I think it's more important for me to stay here and take care of those dogs." April shifted uncomfortably. "To be honest, I really don't know anyone."

Megan understood her position. "I know exactly what you mean, but you know me and my friends if you change your mind. You can sit with us."

"I appreciate that, Megan. Maybe next year, but I'm happy to just get used to everything at the clinic for now."

"Okay, if you change your mind, please call me," Megan said, looking around. "I'd like to pay my bill but I'm not sure where to go."

April laughed. "There's no bill for you. It's your grant that keeps this clinic going so it's our pleasure to serve."

"I don't know about that, but I'll talk to Teddy." Megan gave the dog's leash a slight tug. "Let's go, Dudley. We have to get you home."

April walked them to the door. "Remember, if you see any strange behavior, please call me."

"I will," Megan said. "Believe me, I will."

CHAPTER 43

*N*ick walked into the police station and headed straight into Davis's office. He grabbed the first chair he found, lifted all the papers that had been occupying the seat, and placed them on the desk as he sat down.

"It's about time," Davis said as he pushed the papers to the side.

"I got here as soon as I could." Nick said. "I've got a lot of things going on."

"One of them better be this investigation," Davis said as he leaned back in his chair. "What's going on? Do we have any real leads yet?"

"Nothing much except for the volunteers. Still looking for suspicious background info on them, but haven't come up with much."

"We need to nail one of them to get to the boss. Someone is running the whole show and that's the actor we want."

The two men looked up when Carlos walked into the room. He had a cup of hot coffee in his hand and plopped into another chair right on top of papers and books.

"Hey, watch what your sitting on," Davis yelled at the undercover cop.

"Maybe you should clean this rat hole up on occasion" Carlos said as he drank his coffee.

Davis started to reply but Nick spoke first. "What's going on at the clinic? Are you finding anything we need to look at?"

Carlos shook his head. "Nothing out of the ordinary. I've looked at all the volunteers. The one I'd take a much closer look at is Jared Cooper. The guy couldn't find his way out of a maze if he was given a map and a guide."

Nick started to chuckle but stopped cold when he received a warning look from his boss.

"If he's that dumb, why do you suspect him? Davis asked.

"He's acting weird. He's always looking around. The other thing is the guy is never without the same ratty old scarf around his neck. He's worn it all week. I'm wondering if he's trying to hide something. You know, like a wound?"

"Very interesting," Nick said. "I've seen him in the same scarf but didn't think too much of it."

"Well, I can tell you he never takes it off," Carlos said.

"Maybe he just likes his scarf," Davis said with a shrug. "What does that prove?"

"No, it's more than that, Chief. He acts funny, like he's not feeling well. That scarf is protective for him, like a security blanket."

The Chief looked Carlos in the eye. "Oh, you're a profiler now?"

Carlos shrugged. "Just my opinion. You can take it or leave it. At any rate, there's a lot of things happening there this weekend, so April and I are hanging tight to keep an eye on the place."

Davis turned to Nick. "What about Stokes? Do you have a hospital update?"

"I spoke to the doctor this morning. They'll be backing off the meds soon to take him out of the coma. With any luck, he'll be able to tell us who shot him."

"Is the guard still on his room?"

"Yes, we'll keep him there for a couple more days in case anyone has been waiting to see if he'll talk."

"Good," Davis nodded.

"Did anything come back from the crime scene investigators?" Carlos asked.

Davis thought for a moment. "Yes and no. We didn't get any fingerprints, or I should say we got plenty of fingerprints but none that were out of the ordinary. However, ballistics finally came back with a match on the bullet. It was used for another shooting related to narcotics last year. Interestingly enough, those narcotics were stolen from a veterinarian as well. At minimum, it links these hits in some way. This was not a random robbery or shooting."

"Well then let's hope Dr. Stokes can tell us where to start," Nick said with a shrug.

Davis picked up some of the papers on his desk and threw them back down again as he sighed. "I've got work to do. Both of you need to get the hell out of my office."

Nick started laughing as he stood and followed Sanchez out the door.

CHAPTER 44

*M*egan woke Saturday morning and turned to find Dudley was not in the bed. She sat up and looked around the room. He was lying on the rug, his back against the wall. He had his head down on the floor. Smokey was lying in a tight ball, curved into Dudley's belly.

"Hey, how are you feeling?" Megan asked, not sure if she was expecting an answer. Dudley raised his head a few inches and his tail thumped in response to her voice. "You need to go out?"

Megan hopped out of the bed and in her pajamas walked Dudley downstairs. Smokey raced along behind them, the bell on his collar tinkling as he moved.

Opening the front door, Megan paused to get a coat. Dudley raced outside to the weeds and appeared to make it there just in time to relieve himself. He slowly padded back to the house and in through the front door. The trio then went into the kitchen, but Dudley was not interested in water or food. "I feel really bad for you." She squatted and pet his head. "This is why I wouldn't make a good mommy for dogs. I don't know what I'm doing. I'm sorry."

Dudley looked up with big sad eyes, then laid his head back down on the floor.

Megan had finished making coffee and toast when she heard a knock on the back door. She looked through the window and saw Nick outside.

"Hey, I stopped by to say hi." He placed a bag of donuts on the table and a carrier with two cups of coffee.

"Oh, I just made a pot, but I'll save that for my next cup," Megan said as she picked up the paper cup and started drinking. "Sorry I'm not dressed, but I wanted to get Dudley outside as soon as I could." She used her hands to try to smooth her hair.

"Is he okay?"

"I was in town square watching the tree go up and some little boy fed him a very dark chocolate brownie. I had April check him and he seemed okay, but she said symptoms could last 72 hours. If he were a smaller dog, he could be dead now. I feel so bad that it happened."

"Well what were you doing?"

Megan's face flushed as she realized she was talking to Jonathan. She shrugged and said, "I was watching them put a twenty-five-foot tree into the base at town square. I should have been more attentive to the dog."

"That's the problem with kids and animals. They don't always come with instructions."

Dudley let out a large sigh and they both laughed.

"Nick, are you coming to the Christmas party tonight?"

He shook his head. "Sorry, but I can't. I'm on duty. Normally this town closes in the winter but as we get more permanent residents we need more officers on patrol. One of the guys is out so I'm taking extra shifts. We're asking for another officer, but it has to go through the town budget." Nick took a large gulp of his coffee. "Just in case you have any influence, put in a good word there, will you?"

Megan frowned as she looked at him. "As soon as the holidays are over, I'll start to review what I'm responsible for, so I don't think I can help you now."

Nick shrugged. "Worth a shot, right?"

Megan walked around the table to refill her cup without saying anything.

"So, you'll be at the party tonight?" Nick asked as he watched her pour.

"Yes, Georgie and Amber are coming here and we're all driving to the party together."

"Where is it?"

"I think it's at the Grand Palace," Megan said as she watched Nick snag a chocolate donut out of the paper bag. "You know, that wedding place out on Route 35?"

"Yeah, I haven't been there in a long time, but I've heard it's nice. A lot of big businesses hold their holiday parties there." Nick took the last bite of his donut. "Does it bother you the party was arranged with Stanford Grant money without your knowledge?"

Megan paused and considered Nick's question. "Right now, I don't think so because I do trust Teddy. I'm sure Grandma Rose gave her blessing last year and I would never step in the way of her wishes, but I see I'm going to have to be involved to know what's going on with all that money. Tonight, would be a good start to meet everyone that's associated with a Stanford Grant."

"I'm sure it'll be interesting," Nick said as he finished his coffee.

"I met a few people when Teddy read the will, but I can barely remember them. I was so upset that day." Megan took a sip of her coffee and looked out the back window. "I miss her so much. I feel bad she was alone here the last years of her life. I really thought she was in a better place than she was."

"Hey, you gotta live your life," Nick said as he put his arm around Megan's shoulders. "Your grandmother had a good life but that's why we can't take any day for granted. You just never know."

"Well, thanks for cheering me up," Megan said as she leaned against him. Nick squeezed her shoulders and gave her a kiss on top of her head.

"Listen, I've got to go. Have a good time tonight and I'll call you later."

"Okay," Megan said with a small pout. "Be safe out there, okay?"

"I promise," Nick said as he threw his cup in the garbage and bounded out the door.

CHAPTER 45

The day flew by as Megan ran errands and got ready for the party. Dudley didn't feel up to traveling with her, so he stayed home. Luckily, Marie had come to do some cleaning over the weekend and agreed to watch him while Megan was gone.

Early in the day, Amber called to see what Megan was wearing to the party. When Megan told her she wanted to wear the same outfit she had worn to the Portside, Amber had a faux heart attack. "You can't wear the same outfit."

"Why not? It's very pretty," Megan said.

"Hasn't this party been set up by Teddy and Ellen?"

"Yes, through instructions from Grandma Rose," Megan explained.

"Is it too much to assume that Jonathan will be there?"

"I'm sure he'll be there. He mentioned it the other day."

"Then how in hell can you wear the same thing you wore to dinner the other night? We picked out a couple of dresses. You have to wear something different."

"Okay, calm down," Megan said as they spent the next thirty minutes discussing her wardrobe choices until Amber was satisfied with the outfit she picked.

"I'll be there an hour early, so we can do your makeup and hair."

"I don't want to be too made up," Megan complained.

"This Christmas party is for everyone involved in a Stanford Grant and will probably be a true memorial to your grandmother. I'm sure there will be photos and I know you want to look great, so please let me help you with this."

Megan realized Amber was right and agreed to meet early. Having finished her errands, she went into the kitchen to grab a quick cup of tea before she showered. She found Dudley on the floor and he barely raised his head to look at her. His sad eyes broke her heart. Megan looked at Marie. "Has he had anything to drink or eat?"

Marie shook her head. "He's not interested. I tried several times. Maybe he'll drink for you."

Megan sat on the floor with the dog and tried to encourage him to drink, but he turned his head. She petted him and placed a little bit of water on his tongue hoping he'd want more, but he didn't. His nose and tongue were very dry, but he rested his head on her knee and sighed.

"What do you want me to do if he gets worse?" Marie asked as she looked at the dog.

"Call my cell right away and I'll call April. She said she's hanging around the clinic for most of the day. I tried to get her to come to the dinner. She refused, but I know she'll see Dudley if she needs to."

"Okay, you got it, but don't worry. I'll take good care of him."

Megan got up and picked up her tea. "I know you will, Marie, and thank you."

An hour later, Megan stepped out of the shower. She was in her robe when the doorbell rang followed by the sound of someone running up the stairs. Amber knocked before she ran into the bedroom. She was carrying several shawls and wraps on hangers and had a large bag over her shoulder.

"What's all that?" Megan asked as she watched Amber unload everything.

"I thought one of these wraps might look good with the other dresses we picked up. Plus, I brought my makeup bag, so I can do both of us together."

"Sounds like a lot of work."

"Let's just get your outfit ready and match things up," Amber said as she opened the closet door and began to rifle through the clothes.

When Georgie arrived fifteen minutes later, Megan was seated in front of a makeup mirror and Amber was curling her hair. "Hey, glad you could join us," Megan said as she teased Georgie.

"Let me look at your outfit," Amber directed as she made Georgie twirl. "You actually look hot in that dress."

Georgie threw a pillow at Amber who deflected it with her hand.

"You want me to check your makeup?" Amber asked.

"It's up to you," Georgie said. "I don't know if you'll have time between you and Megan."

"Very funny," Amber said as she stuck her tongue out at Georgie.

Megan rolled her eyes in the mirror and watched her friends spar behind her. When they finished, Georgie turned to Megan. "What's the status with the walk and the tree lighting?"

"As you know, Ellen got the permits which is why Nora made sure the tree was delivered right away. I watched yesterday when they put it in the stand in town square. Hopefully, some families have already started hanging decorations. I'm donating the money for generic ornaments, but we'll need a lot more."

"That sounds great," Georgie said. "We'll make sure we get the word out on social media. When is the actual tree lighting?"

"It's scheduled for next Sunday," Megan said with a smile. "We'll start the Ocean Holiday Walk at 6:00 p.m., then have the tree lighting and Christmas carols at 7:30 p.m." She turned to Amber. "Is Tommy all set up to play?"

"Tommy and the Tides will be there, wearing Christmas hats and playing Christmas songs. He's bringing everything they need except an electric outlet. If they have somewhere to plug in, they'll be ready to go at 7:00 p.m. They planned on playing some background music as people filter in."

"What about the tables, Georgie?"

"I've got twelve tables being set up," Georgie said. "The rest of the committee members have been very helpful. Several tables will have food and the others will have crafts for sale. We'll have hot chocolate, tea, coffee, candy canes, and cookies. There will be an extra table for anyone who wants to bring a dessert. Let's see, the craft tables that have already registered will have ornaments, Christmas decorations, candles, hand sewn and crocheted items. There are other tables registering as well and don't forget photos with Santa Claus."

"This is really exciting," Megan said.

"Can we have an official Jingle Bell Run next year in combination with the Ocean Holiday Walk? It could be a 5K Run which would be a fundraiser," Georgie said excitedly. "I'll be point person for that project, but I'd have to start planning now. We'd need to map out the course, print up t-shirts and get sponsors. We'd have to get volunteers. Some of the lifeguards are paramedics so they'd help. I'd love to plan it like a regular run, but with the holiday theme. Of course, we'd have to get a group to run dressed like Santa and his reindeer."

"Hey, take a breath." Megan laughed while Amber rolled her eyes.

An hour later, when they were all finally ready, they said goodbye to Dudley, Smokey and Marie and left for the Christmas party.

CHAPTER 46

The room was cold. Jared pulled his chair up to a table covered with pizza boxes and dirty paper towel as Micky gathered the equipment he needed in a small bag. "You're going to have to focus tonight," Micky said as he picked up a set of lock picks. "It's bad enough I have to go, I don't need you screwing it up."

"I'll focus but I still have a fever," Jared complained. "And I'm dizzy."

"Listen, after tonight, drive anywhere you want, preferably far out of state and get some drugs. You're driving me crazy. I'll send you your cut, just get out." Micky threw a small hammer in the bag. He shook his head with frustration.

"Are we leaving soon? Everyone will be at that party," Jared said as he looked up at the clock.

"We'll wait awhile," Micky said. "Just in case they go to the party late. I'd rather go around 2:00 a.m. Less chance we'll run into anyone and hopefully they'll all be drunk by that time."

Micky looked at Jared and kicked his foot. "You have six hours to kill, go take some aspirin and a nap. Then one last job and we're out of here. The boss promised me we'll move to another state and as far as I'm concerned, the sooner the better."

"I hope so, Micky. I don't want to go to jail and I don't want to die."

CHAPTER 47

*M*egan pulled up to the valet at the Grand Palace. Several young men ran to open the doors of the car, so the women could hop out. Megan handed over her key and received a numbered tag. The valet hopped in the car and drove away as the women turned toward the door.

The lobby was made of marble, and adorned with twinkling lights. Christmas decorations were everywhere, and the scent of evergreen, cinnamon and freshly baked cookies filled the air. They turned toward their right and handed their coats to the clerk.

The trio walked straight ahead and found a table laden with small ceramic stockings. Each stocking had a name written on it and next to the name was a table number.

"Hey, Megan, here's your stocking," Amber said as she handed it to her. "Number one."

"And here are ours," Georgie said as she handed a ceramic stocking to Amber. "We're also at table number one."

"I hope that's a good table," Megan said as they entered the ball room. Colored lights painted the walls and each table had lit candles sitting within a fragrant wreath. A band was set up against the wall in the center of the room. Tables were covered with red and green linens and had Christmas china and small presents in front of each chair.

"Here it is," Amber sang out as they found the table. The three women claimed seats and placed their purses on their chairs.

Within seconds, they were approached by a waitress carrying a tray with appetizers. "Care for shrimp cocktail?" She handed each of them a napkin as they choose a toothpick containing a large piece of shrimp.

"I think I'm really going to like this party," Georgie said as she popped the appetizer in her mouth. She then followed the shrimp with a cocktail hot dog, stuffed mushroom, coconut chicken, grilled scallop and a piece of cranberry crostini.

Amber watched with horror. "If that were me, I'd have to stop eating for the next three days."

"Or you could run fifteen miles tomorrow morning and not worry about it," Georgie countered.

"Good evening, you all look beautiful," Jonathan said as he approached the ladies and handed Megan a flute of champagne. Megan was happy Amber had picked a sparkling Ralph Lauren cold-shoulder cocktail dress for her to wear. "I'm sorry I didn't have enough hands to bring champagne for everyone," he said as he looked at her friends.

"Jonathan, please meet Amber and Georgie," Megan said as she introduced her friends.

"Pleased to meet you," Jonathan said as he gave a slight bow. He stopped a waiter who was passing by and procured two more glasses of champagne for Amber and Georgie.

They murmured their thanks and sipped the bubbly liquid as he turned back to Megan.

"You really do look gorgeous tonight," Jonathan said. He turned and gestured toward the room. "I hope you're pleased with the result. We tried to do our very best to honor your grandmother."

Looking around the room, Megan said, "It's beautiful, Jonathan, and I really appreciate all the effort you went to." Amber and Georgie rolled their eyes at one another and stepped to the side as Teddy and

Ellen approached the table. There were air kisses and hugs all around as Megan introduced her friends.

"We're all sitting at the head table," Teddy said as he placed his glass on the table. "Why don't we make ourselves comfortable?"

Jonathan waited until the women were all seated. Amber and Georgie made sure Megan sat to their left with Jonathan by her side followed by Teddy and Ellen. They were joined by four more people who introduced themselves to Megan as Executive Directors of some of the charities the fund supported.

The group chatted for thirty minutes and after most of the guests arrived, Teddy walked up to the podium and began to welcome everyone. He spoke of how proud he was of all the guests in the room who had worked so selflessly over the year to support and carry out the work the charity funded.

He continued, "In order to honor the woman who has given us the gift and insight to create the Stanford Grants and to give you an idea of the impact of your challenging work, dedication and compassion, we've prepared a video for you to watch. If you would please direct your attention to the screen," Teddy said as he pointed behind him.

The group spent the next ten minutes watching a film about the life of Rose Stanford which segued into shots and testimonies of persons helped by the grant, offering their thanks and well wishes to the Stanford family.

Megan sat at the table and watched as tears flowed down her cheeks, especially when there was footage of her grandmother helping at the animal clinic, or hospital or library. Jonathan reached over and held her around the shoulders again. He pulled out a pristine handkerchief and handed it to her. The video ended with a large photo of a smiling, vibrant Rose Stanford. The standing ovation lasted a full five minutes.

Before he went back to the podium, Teddy asked if he could introduce Megan to the crowd. She nodded yes, but asked for a moment to wipe her face. Amber leaned over to Georgie and said, "Thankfully, I used the waterproof mascara."

The applause again lasted several minutes when Teddy introduced

Megan as Rose's granddaughter but more importantly, the family member who would manage the Stanford Grants moving forward. Megan was overwhelmed with the emotion of the night and vowed to continue her grandmother's work after seeing the impact it made on the community at large.

After more applause, Megan returned to the table to receive hugs from everyone there. She shook a little as she sat, and Jonathan held her hands until she calmed. Within minutes, the waiters served a delicious meal followed by luscious desserts and coffee.

During the evening, many people introduced themselves to Megan. She tried to make rounds of the tables but was held up by a receiving line for her near the podium. As the crowd began to thin, Georgie pulled her aside and pushed her cell phone into her hand. "I think you should answer this. Marie has called several times, so it may be important."

Megan bit her lip as she placed the phone to her ear. "Hello?"

"Megan, it's Marie. I really hate to bother you tonight, but I think you should come home and call April. Dudley doesn't look well and he's acting funny. Almost like he's nauseous and disoriented."

"Oh no, we'll leave right away," Megan said. "I'll call her on the way, so we can run in and put him in the car."

"Alright, we'll be ready when you get here."

Megan excused herself and ran back to the table. She explained the situation and grabbed her purse. Jonathan walked her to the lobby and handed her car tag to the valet. "Would you like me to come with you and help?"

She refused his offer when the girls promised to go with her. "Stay with the crowd and offer my apologies. I'd appreciate that."

"As you wish," Jonathan said as her car arrived. The valet opened the doors. Jonathan walked her to the driver's side and handed the valet some money. Before he handed her into the car, he said, "I hope you were pleased with the presentation and I'm looking forward to working with you." He smiled and kissed her on the cheek. After helping her into the car, he waited until she had her seat belt on before closing the door.

Her friends were silent as she drove. "Stop it," Megan yelled.

"Stop what?" Amber asked. "We're not saying a thing."

"That's exactly my point," Megan said as she shifted gears and headed home.

CHAPTER 48

When they arrived at Misty Manor, Megan parked as close as she could to the house. She had called April who immediately agreed to go back to the clinic and see Dudley. Georgie and Megan helped Dudley get into the car. Amber was pulled away when she received a call from her girlfriend who had a little too much to drink and asked if Amber could pick her up and drive her home.

Megan sped to the animal clinic while Georgie watched Dudley in the back seat. They went to the back door where April asked to meet them. When they knocked, she immediately opened the door and let them in. She guided them to the exam room and closed the door as the group crowded in. She lowered the exam table with an electronic pedal and they placed Dudley on the surface. "Will he be okay?" Megan asked nervously as she watched April work on him. She looked in his eyes and checked his nose and tongue. She took his temperature and listened to his heart and lungs.

"Has he had anything to eat or drink since the chocolate?"

"Nothing much," Megan said. "I tried to put water right on his tongue, but he didn't seem interested."

"Hmm, the chocolate should be out of his system already. Sometimes we use charcoal to absorb the toxin and it's a bit late for that, but I don't think it would hurt to try. He's dehydrated so he'll need an IV as well."

"Whatever you think," Megan said. "Just help him, please."

"Let me see if we have charcoal in the supply room. I put everything we have in the safe and I just can't remember if that was in the shipment."

"Okay," Megan said. She looked at Georgie with a worried expression as April left to open the safe. A few minutes went by and April hadn't returned yet.

"She's taking a long time, isn't she?" Georgie asked as she looked at her watch.

"Maybe she's having trouble finding it," Megan said as she shrugged her shoulders. She turned back to Dudley and petted his head. "He feels hot to me."

Another minute went by. "Maybe I'll check to see if I can help her," Megan said as she opened the door. "You stay with Dudley." Megan took a step toward the main room and the opened door. She then realized the area outside the exam room was pitch black. She turned back toward Georgie and whispered, "Weren't those lights on when we came in here?"

"Damn straight they were," Georgie whispered back. "Why would she turn them off?"

"I have no idea," Megan said. "Something seems very wrong here."

Megan took a small step outside the door to look around. Before she took another step, she felt something cold in the back of her neck and heard a click. "Don't move."

Georgie had taken out her cell phone and typed the word "help" but before she had a chance to hit send, she heard a voice say, "Put down that cell phone or I'll blow your friend here away."

She looked up to see a man march Megan back into the exam room with a gun to her head.

"Oh my God," Georgie said. "Don't hurt her."

"You know, it's a shame because everything had gone so well tonight. We came in, we got the fancy dogs, cracked the safe and were all ready to go. I cannot believe you had to walk in here with that dog. Truly a shame because you'll all have to die now."

"Where's April?" Megan said as she made eye movements toward Georgie.

"She's deep in dreamland now," Micky said. "The room was dark when she came out, so she didn't have to die, but unfortunately, you've seen our face."

"We won't tell anyone, I swear," Megan said, trembling as she looked around the room.

"Sorry, but I don't believe you." His fingers bit into the flesh of her upper arm.

"You're hurting me. You don't have to do this," Megan said as she turned to her left, hoping to get the man to move with her.

He held the gun up. "Let's skip the dance and get this over with." He gestured for Georgie to move.

While he was distracted, Megan reached her fingers slightly to the side and grabbed a defibrillator paddle spoon without him noticing. She made a face at Georgie hoping she would understand her direction to cause a distraction.

"She swore not to tell anyone and when she swears to something, she means it," Georgie said, backing toward the other side of the room.

"Don't move," Micky said as he pointed the gun toward Georgie for a moment. While his attention was diverted, Megan swung the defibrillator paddle and hit Micky in the face with it. Grabbing his eye, he dropped the gun and the girls ran toward the outer room. Georgie cleared the door, but before Megan got there, she felt a hard tug on the back of her clothes. She was pulled backwards and slammed to the floor. Micky slapped her across the face to make her stay down as he lunged across the floor to find the gun.

Georgie screamed from the outer room when Jared grabbed her wrist. Without hesitating, she turned around and slammed her fist in Jared's stomach. He grunted and fell to the floor. She kicked him several times and tried to run away but his hand grabbed her around the ankle. She lost her balance and fell to the floor as well.

Micky found his gun and stood up. "You've made the biggest mistake of your life, bitch."

"I don't know. It felt pretty good to me," Megan said as she laughed and put a hand up to her cheek which throbbed with pain.

"I hope you laugh on your way to hell," Micky said as he raised the gun and pointed it at Megan's head.

Out of nowhere, Dudley lunged off the table and grabbed Micky around the wrist with his strong jaws. Despite the screams, Dudley would not let go of the man's arm. As his teeth ripped into the vessels and flesh of Micky's wrist, the gun wavered back and forth. The gun blasts hurt their ears as bullets ricocheted around the room. Glass jars and pieces of wall exploded as they were hit.

Dudley looked deranged as he lunged on top of Micky when he hit the floor and bit into his shoulder. Micky's screams were muffled by Dudley's paws pushing down on his larynx. Megan continued screaming as the gun dropped to the floor and she watched in horror.

Jared rose from the floor in the outside room and yanked Georgie to her feet. He was about to punch her when Carlos lunged forward and tackled Jared to the floor again. With one punch across the face, Jared went limp and was unconscious.

Nick ran into the exam room and found Megan, Micky and Dudley lying on the floor in a pool of blood. His stomach knotted, he ran to Megan who opened her eyes and began to cry.

CHAPTER 49

*M*egan woke up and groaned. Within seconds, Nick was at her side, trying to keep her calm.

He had waited by her side for the ambulance, his feelings alternating between anger and fear that she'd been shot. One by one, the emergency technicians loaded everyone into rigs and sent them to Coastal Community. They picked Dudley up and placed him back on the hospital emergency table. The police searched the entire building and found April in the supply closet. She had been knocked unconscious and was locked in the room.

Other officers had canvassed the cars on the street and found the two dogs. A bag of narcotics was near Jared's body when they picked him up to arrest him. He was also sent to the hospital to be treated.

"Hey, relax. You're okay, I'm here with you."

"Where am I?" Megan said as she looked around, dazed from her sleep and massive headache.

"You're in the emergency room of Coastal Community." Nick reached down and hugged Megan as best as he could as she lay on the gurney. "You have a bad bruise to your face, but the doc said you're going to be okay. I thought you'd been shot but you weren't."

"What about everyone else? Georgie? Dudley? April?" Megan asked, fear rising in her chest.

"Georgie was examined and released about an hour ago. She's going to be okay." Nick said.

"And April?"

"She'll be okay, too. Those guys had knocked her out and locked her in the supply closet. Other than a bump on her head, she'll be fine."

Megan looked into Nick's face to see what he was holding back from her. "What else? Nick tell me, what else?"

"There was a guy named Jared. He was the guy who grabbed Georgie. He's also the volunteer who shot Dr. Stokes a week ago. Dr. Stokes managed to stab him in the neck with a scalpel before he was shot. The guy hid a disgusting, festering wound all week and will be lucky if he doesn't die from sepsis, but Carlos took him out as he was trying to hurt Georgie."

"How did you know where we were?"

"I figured the Christmas party was over, so I stopped by the house to see how it went. Carlos and I had been at the hospital talking to Dr. Stokes who told us about Jared. There's someone else involved, but we don't know who it is yet. That's who we want, the gang leader." Nick paused and sighed. "We wanted to warn you. When we got to the house, Marie told us you were at the clinic. When you didn't answer your phone, I raced to the clinic because I had a bad feeling and unfortunately I was right."

Megan fell back on her gurney and put her hand to her cheek. "What about the other guy?"

"He's not doing well. His name is Micky. Seems he got off some shots in that exam room. The bullets ricocheted all over. I thought he caught a few, but it seems he was attacked by Dudley when he tried to shoot you. Dudley ripped up his wrist as well as his shoulder pretty bad."

"But Dudley was so sick," Megan said. "He was lying on the table."

Nick looked down and softly stroked her hair. "Well, it seems he gathered what little strength he had left to protect you. He saved your life, Megan."

"Where is he now?" Megan immediately teared up, her head pounded as she tried to sit up. Fear gripped her heart. "Where's Dudley?"

Nick held her hand, gently pushed her back on the gurney and smiled. "He's resting. They got the county vet to come to the clinic. He put in an IV and cleaned him up. Luckily, he wasn't shot either. Apparently, all the blood on the floor belonged to Micky."

CHAPTER 50

The next week flew by. Megan remained a guest of Coastal Community for one night as they ordered fluids, pain killers and a CT scan for her head. The results of the CT scan were normal despite protests from her friends. She spent the next couple of days at Misty Manor on advice from her doctor to rest and let her injuries heal.

During that time, Nora sent a beautiful Christmas tree to Misty Manor which was set up by Nick near the fireplace in the solarium. When Megan felt well enough, she and Nick retrieved the vintage ornaments from the third floor and decorated. Afterward, they sat on the couch, warmed by the fire, watching the ocean and admiring the tree.

Over the next couple of days, Megan received visits from her friends as well as gifts and well wishes from the community. Teddy, Ellen and Jonathan all stopped by to see how she was doing and sent a gorgeous gift basket of fruit.

April was released from the hospital almost immediately and went back to work at the Hand in Paws Animal Clinic.

Plans were made and remade and finally the night of the Ocean Holiday Walk arrived.

"I'm glad it's a beautiful day," Megan said as she readied herself with the crowd.

"Yes, that's the problem with having this walk in Winter. It could have been snowing with a cold blustery wind," said Amber as she wrapped her designer exercise clothes around her body.

"You got a nice crowd though," said Georgie. "A lot of residents and visitors so I'd say it was a success already." Raising a megaphone, Georgie declared an official start to the walk and the group of people began the one mile walk down the boardwalk. Some of the walkers made notes as they went along to properly judge the best decorations contest. They walked by the hotels, the stores, and coffee shops which were all fully decorated, open and full of patrons.

The town had made a special effort to decorate the posts on the boardwalk with garland and bows. Christmas Songs rang out from speakers as they made their way along the ocean. When they reached the end of the boardwalk, the group stopped to admire the decorations on Misty Manor before they exited onto Ocean Ave and continued forward.

"The house looks absolutely fantastic this year," Georgie said as they passed. "Misty Manor hasn't seen that amount of Christmas cheer in a long time. You and Nick did a fantastic job decorating."

"Same for the town in general," Amber said. "The morale is the highest it's been in years."

As they approached the next curve in Ocean Ave, they veered right and walked into the middle of the town square. As promised, Tommy and the Tides were playing music from a bandstand in the corner of the square. A voice on a loudspeaker announced the walkers as they came in. They passed by a table and were given a cup of hot chocolate and a homemade sprinkle cookie.

"You guys did a hell of a job planning this fundraiser," Megan said.

"Just wait until next year after we have some real time to organize things," Georgie said with a nod.

"And I didn't get a chance to tell you, but my philanthropy group at work is going to match whatever funds you raise tonight," Amber added with a wink.

"I am truly floored with your efforts," Megan said. "Thank you."

"It's all for a worthy cause," the women agreed as they ate their cookies.

Megan and her friends gathered in the square to await the rest of the festivities where they were joined by Nick and Carlos. Nick put his arm around Megan and kissed her on top of the head. Carlos began to chat with Georgie and Amber while they watched Tommy play music.

"Hey, how are you feeling?" Nick asked as they faded into the crowd.

"Fine, the throbbing has almost completely gone away," she said as she took another bite of her cookie.

"So, I've been dying to know. How did you two make out?" Megan asked.

Nick grinned. "I guess I can tell you now as all the arrests have been made. As you know, the night you went to the clinic, Dr. Stokes was brought out of his coma and able to tell us that Jared was the person who shot him. Dr. Stokes knew about some petty thefts but didn't want to upset anyone until he had more information."

"How is he doing?" Megan asked.

"It appears the surgery was a success, but he has a long road ahead of him with therapy."

"I'll have to stop by and visit," Megan said. "But go on."

"Okay, while Jared was in the hospital, he was told he was going to jail for a long time. He broke down and started singing like a canary about their little gang and their plan to target various animal clinics and shelters for the narcotics, supplies and valuable animals. They'd sell them or redistribute for cash and then move on to another county when things got too hot in each area. This heist was to be their last. They probably would have gotten away with everything if you didn't need to bring Dudley to the clinic."

Megan felt a knot in her stomach at the mention of the dog.

"You're never going to believe who the ringleader of the group was," Nick said as he smiled.

"Out with it then. Who was it?"

"Turns out that Judy Bowan's real name is Jane Cooper." Nick laughed when he saw Megan's expression. "That's right, Miss Dimples herself. Her background check as Judy Bowan didn't show anything but when we ran her prints her record came up. She's Jared's mother and has been a scam artist for quite a long time. She'd go into a shelter, establish herself as a solid volunteer and earn their trust. Eventually, she'd have access to supplies, drugs and everything else. As time went by, she got Jared and Micky to do the dirty work. They'd split the proceeds and eventually move on."

"Don't these places check their volunteers?" Megan asked.

"Not all of them and not as thoroughly as they're supposed to. That's why some of the rules surrounding volunteer work are changing."

"So, what happens next with Mrs. Cooper?"

"That's the best part," Nick said with a smile. "She was just arrested and brought into headquarters for questioning. Using her proper name, fingerprints and intel from Jared, we've been able to build quite a file. She'll become a guest in the county jail until this is all handled properly, but they're all going down. You've helped to break up a narcotics ring although I am over the hill pissed you almost got killed again."

"Hey, I didn't go out and ask for it," Megan insisted as she finished her hot chocolate.

"I know, but I'm thinking of locking you in Misty Manor for the rest of your life to keep you out of trouble. Knowing you, you'll find even more trouble there to get involved in."

"Hey, you gotta live your life, right? I believe you're the one who told me that," Megan mocked.

"Point taken," Nick said as he gave her a hug and kiss. "I've got to get back to work but I'll see you later."

Megan searched his eyes. "I'm looking forward to it, Nick."

As he walked away, Megan joined her friends near the tree to wait for the lights to be turned on. She hugged Nora and the kids who were eating treats and filled with laughter.

Teddy, Ellen and Jonathan came over and exchanged holiday hugs and kisses. Jonathan hugged her for a moment longer than necessary and told her they would arrange lunch after the holidays to start talking about the grant in earnest and she agreed.

Megan turned when someone tapped her on the shoulder and found April behind her, holding a leash. She had to let go when Dudley jumped into the waiting arms of Megan. They hugged as Dudley went nuts licking her face and leaning against her. Megan fell over and laughed as the dog landed on top of her and wouldn't move. After April finally pulled Megan to her feet, she said, "You had your chance to bring his bowl back while he was in the shelter."

"Never. I won't give up Dudley," Megan said as she continued to pet his head. "I'll learn to be a better fur mommy to take care of him forever and Smokey is waiting for him at home."

"He's feeling a lot better and they are officially all yours now," April said with a smile as she handed Megan an envelope of papers.

"I'm the luckiest person in the square right now, aren't I?"

Megan smiled as she heard the final countdown by the crowd. Four, three, two, one.. and the magnificent tree lit up filled with colored lights and sparkling ornaments. The group clapped and swayed together as they sang Christmas songs in the beautiful ocean breeze.

ABOUT THE AUTHOR

Linda Rawlins is an American writer of mystery fiction best known for her Misty Point Mystery Series, including Misty Manor and Misty Point. She is also known for her Rocky Meadow Mystery Series, including The Bench, Fatal Breach and Sacred Gold. She loved to read as a child and started writing her first mystery novel in fifth grade. She then went on to study science, medicine and literature, eventually graduating medical school and establishing her career in medicine.

Linda Rawlins lives in New Jersey with her husband, her family and spoiled pets. She loves spending time at the beach as well as visiting the mountains of Vermont.

Tell me how you liked my book!

lindarawlins.com